MW01061690

## "I was running on

"Thanks, by the way, for tucking me in and staying with me."

Abi had never needed that before from anyone, so she was certain it wouldn't happen again.

"Not a problem," Grayson said, but his husky voice told a slightly different story. Was he as affected by her as she was by him? There'd been a few signs here and there, but she almost convinced herself she was reading too much into them. Maybe even seeing what she wanted to see versus what was there. But the sound of his voice and the look in his eyes told a different story.

They said the attraction was mutual.

Not that it mattered. They lived in different cities. He had a kid. They had different lives.

And after this case, they would have no reason to talk.

# CAPTURED IN
# WEST TEXAS

## BARB HAN

**Harlequin**

**INTRIGUE**

If you purchased this book without a cover you should be aware that this
book is stolen property. It was reported as "unsold and destroyed" to the
publisher, and neither the author nor the publisher has received any
payment for this "stripped book."

All my love to Brandon, Jacob and Tori, my three greatest loves.
To Samantha, welcome to the family officially. Happy first
anniversary. I love you all more than words!

To Babe, my hero, for being my best friend, my greatest love and
my place to call home. I love you with everything that I am.

And, last but certainly not least, to Oliver and
Birgit Pohl for a rare and beautiful friendship.

 Harlequin®
INTRIGUE™

Recycling programs
for this product may
not exist in your area.

ISBN-13: 978-1-335-45726-4

Captured in West Texas

Copyright © 2025 by Barb Han

All rights reserved. No part of this book may be used or reproduced in any manner
whatsoever without written permission.

Without limiting the author's and publisher's exclusive rights, any unauthorized use of
this publication to train generative artificial intelligence (AI) technologies is expressly
prohibited.

This is a work of fiction. Names, characters, places and incidents are either the
product of the author's imagination or are used fictitiously. Any resemblance to
actual persons, living or dead, businesses, companies, events or locales is entirely
coincidental.

For questions and comments about the quality of this book, please contact us at
CustomerService@Harlequin.com.

TM and ® are trademarks of Harlequin Enterprises ULC.

 Harlequin Enterprises ULC
22 Adelaide St. West, 41st Floor
Toronto, Ontario M5H 4E3, Canada
www.Harlequin.com

Printed in U.S.A.

*USA TODAY* bestselling author **Barb Han** lives in north Texas with her very own hero-worthy husband, three beautiful children, a spunky golden retriever/standard poodle mix and too many books in her to-read pile. In her downtime, she plays video games and spends much of her time on or around a basketball court. She loves interacting with readers and is grateful for their support. You can reach her at barbhan.com.

Visit the Author Profile page at Harlequin.com.

## CAST OF CHARACTERS

*Abilene Remington*—Can this US marshal stop a serial killer before he strikes again?

*Grayson Chisolm*—Will this FBI agent's heart survive losing another person he loves, and can he risk his child's life when the case hits a little too close to home?

*Reynosa the Reprehensible*—What is this brutal murderer's real identity, and can he be stopped?

*Max Hague*—Does this sole survivor of a serial killer hold the key to unlock the case?

*Deputy Thad Carlson*—Is this law enforcement officer's judgment being clouded, and will his sloppy investigation allow a serial killer to get away with murder?

*Sheriff Benton*—How much can this sheriff be trusted?

# Chapter One

Abilene Remington, Abi to everyone who knew her, cursed her family tree as she squeezed the piercing pinch in her side and tried to catch her breath. Genetics had given her five feet two inches of height, which meant she had short legs. She was fast, like soccer players gunning down the pitch about to score fast, but short. Also, she hated running. She'd never liked it. Never wanted to be a runner despite Mesa Point High School coach David McGeary's burning desire to put her on the team. But running was as much part of a US marshal's job as sharpshooting. Felons who were about to be sentenced to life in prison or worse didn't have a whole lot to lose. So they ran, or they fired a weapon, or both, sometimes at the same time.

Reynosa the Reprehensible, the felon she'd chased to the abandoned strip mall, was a runner.

Typical.

Maybe she should change his name to Reynosa the Runner instead.

Abi could think of dozens of better things to do at ten o'clock on a Saturday morning in late October than go for a run, but it would be worth it if the tip was correct, this was actually Reprehensible, and she could take a serial killer off the streets.

Lungs clawing for air, Abi almost skidded to a dead stop in front of an opened industrial AC unit vent. *Are you kidding me?*

Since Abi could keep up with the best of them, she almost always got to places before her colleagues, who were other marshals, deputies or cops. Depending on the case, they might be from one of those other alphabet agencies while on joint task forces. Being short, tiny and small-boned, she also got to be the one to follow perps into tight spaces.

Lucky her.

Abi didn't have time to wait for Agent Grayson Chisolm to catch up. Not if she was going to keep Reynosa the Reprehensible within reach. Catching the bastard was the only way to stop the senseless murders. This twisted offender had cut short the lives of five college kids already and counting. According to the FBI profiler from Quantico assigned to the case, this young male wouldn't stop until he was caught or dead.

Climbing into the abandoned warehouse's AC vent, she took a deep breath to steel her resolve and make herself slim enough to fit into the tiny shaft. The opening wasn't large enough for her to crawl into: she had to go belly down as she stretched her arms out in front of her.

Teeth clenched, Abi did what she'd been hired to do. She climbed inside and went after the felon, hoping to catch him before he got away.

Despite Halloween coming up in a couple of days and the fact the sun hadn't yet reached its peak, the metal vent was stuffy and unusually hot. Dust caused her to sneeze almost immediately. There hadn't been any air circulating in this sucker for a long time. Would she even be able to breathe as she wriggled her way toward Reprehensible?

He was too far ahead to grab. There was at least a slight chance another law enforcement officer or agent would make it around the building to greet him on the other side. The thought kept her pushing him toward the exit.

"Surrender," she commanded in her most authoritative voice. Perps like these rarely listened to her but it was worth a shot. Plus, it was protocol to identify herself. Her voice bounced off the tin walls. She tried to shout above the shuffling noises that made her ears hurt. "My name is Marshal Remington, of the US Marshals Service. I'm ordering you to stop. *Now*!"

*What? Nothing?* Her sarcasm wouldn't exactly win her any originality awards but amused her in stressful times. Staying calm and keeping her focus was critical in clutch situations. Developing a sense of humor about her job kept her from burnout, which had taken a lot of great marshals down before and during her time, her grandfather included. But his heart had always been in the paint horse ranch he'd built from nothing. Sadness at the thought of her grandparent threatened to crack her focus.

At twenty-eight years old, she wasn't ready to throw in the towel in her current profession. In some ways, she was just getting started.

The feeling of a dozen fire ants crawling underneath her skin jacked her pulse through the roof. Being this close to pure evil always affected her in more ways than one. Her skin crawled and bile churned in her stomach. Adrenaline thumped through her veins, pushing her forward and turning her into what her supervisor called Ramped-up Abi. It was her on steroids. Her stubborn streak caused her to dig in her heels. Her version of fast became hyper speed. And when she locked onto a target, she was better than military-grade precision weapons. Her laser-like focus amped up too. Wonder Woman had nothing on Abi when she was this close to catching a creep.

Senses on high alert, she also heard claws against the metal scurrying ahead of her. Mice? Rats?

*Oh, please don't let it be rats this time.* They might be intelligent critters and some folks might enjoy keeping them as pets, but they gave Abi the heebie-jeebies. Every time. Her body rocked an involuntary shudder at the thought of sharing space with them.

"Marshal Remington, you in there?" FBI Agent Grayson Chisolm's deep timbre came through the radio in a low whisper, echoing inside the hollow container. Well, almost hollow. There were two humans army-crawling as fast as they could go, blocking sound's ability to travel to the opposite end. There were critters too, but she forced those out of her mind, or all forward progress would be lost, and she'd end up stuck. Trust her, it happened.

At least Agent Chisolm had finally arrived on the scene. He wasn't as fast a runner as Abi, but the man had arms built like a bodybuilder's and he had a reputation for being the best. This was the first joint task force she'd worked on with him, and she refused to be intimidated by his legendary status.

At the risk of giving her location away again, she whispered a response, "Yes." Then again, climbing through the shaft wasn't exactly quiet. Taking in air through her nose and blowing it out her mouth long and slow was a vain attempt to calm her rapid heartbeat. Swallowing dust and God knew what else in pursuit of Reprehensible wasn't exactly her ideal way of starting her day. Losing him would be much worse, so she doubled down on the army crawls.

There was truly little wiggle room in that air vent. Arms tucked to her sides with barely enough room to crawl, she pressed on. The perp's loud movement up ahead combined with his heavy breathing should hopefully mask most of the noise she was making.

In this tight space it would be next to impossible for him to look back. The longer it took for him to realize she was gaining on him, the better. No matter how fast she went, though, he would reach the opposite end before her. Guaranteed.

At least the space was tight enough to ensure he wouldn't be able to get off a shot while they were both inside, if he had a weapon. Otherwise, she'd be a goner already, because she was directly behind him with nowhere to go. Once he made it out the other end, though…

Too soon, Abi saw a hint of light in front of her, which meant the perp was getting close to the exit. On her belly like a worm, she inched her way toward him, determined not to let him get away. In front of her was nothing but darkness except for the occasional peek of light.

The perp, based on her earlier glimpse of him from a hundred yards away where it was hard to judge, couldn't be a large man. Although, the dark, baggy clothes made it difficult to define his shape. There was no way someone the size of a linebacker would fit in the vent. Agent Chisolm would definitely not be able to squeeze into this tight space.

This man could fit into the vent with Abi, which made him even smaller than the size the FBI profiler who'd been assigned to do a case study had originally believed him to be. These profiles, she'd learned, were always being refined when new information came in.

The perp couldn't be much wider than her. Taller, yes. But not broader. She was almost shoulder to shoulder with the walls.

Abi made mental notes to report back to the team in case this thing went south, and he got away.

*This bastard has to be caught. Period.*

She clawed her way closer to him, but he was still too far out of reach. If only she could close the distance faster.

The first hint he wasn't physically as strong as someone like Chisolm was the fact Reprehensible drugged his victims before torturing and eventually killing them. The murderer didn't rely on brute strength, which had been noted by the profiler. The bodies of all the five college kids he'd already killed had been found in shallow graves in the border town of Reynosa, Mexico, since the semester began late August. All five had brown hair and were reported as last being seen at a party. All victims had been given bowl cuts despite their sex. There'd been two female and three male victims to date. In two months, this bastard had taken five lives, with no sign of slowing down or stopping. The sixth attempt—on nineteen-year-old Max Hague—was the reason the task force believed they had a location on the perp and Abi was presently crawling through this damn vent.

The last thing Max remembered before being drugged was being at a party and drinking. He had managed to escape a structure—he'd said the size of roughly a two-car garage—and run while half-dazed and almost naked to flag down a motorist.

And then a call came in that someone had broken into a detached garage of a boarded-up home five blocks away from the party where Max last remembered being. Max fit the kind of victim Reprehensible thrived on finding. If this was Reprehensible, they had another detail to add to the case file. He took his victims to a secondary location, possibly for days before killing them.

Light filled the vent shaft. Abi tensed, waiting for the crack of a bullet.

Nothing came.

The perp was gone.

Could Abi at least get through fast enough to get a direction before he disappeared?

THE LAST MINUTES of morning were ticking by. At this rate, the perp would be long gone by the time Grayson Chisolm made it around the long strip mall on foot. At forty years old, he was the most experienced member on the joint task force, which also consisted of a US marshal, a sheriff and a deputy from the border town of McAllen, plus members from Texas State University campus PD, University of Texas at Austin campus PD, as well as Austin PD. Including him, the number came up to seven. Sheriff Benton and Deputy Carlson were on the team. It was a decent-sized team that had been formed a few days ago in order to catch the serial killer dubbed Reynosa the Reprehensible by the media.

Grayson wasn't a fan of giving this sonofabitch a name, especially so early in the process. Two months since his killing spree had started, and the body count was already racking up. Giving him a name might inflate his ego, which in turn could ramp up his killing streak.

The perp must have some tie to Reynosa, Mexico, since the bodies were found there, but that didn't mean he was born there, lived there, or worked there like a couple of the task force members had decided. The location might be a convenient place to dump a body since it was across the border from a small Texas town.

Marshal Remington kept an open mind. She'd argued against using the media dub to name the file, same as him. They'd lost on that one, but he was relieved to have someone who thought like him on the team. It was important to size everyone up on a task force like this, to find allies for when the time came to make critical decisions. Having one person on his side had tipped the scale in his favor more than once, if not this time.

Grayson had been on the job long enough to trust his instincts—instincts honed by years of experience. The good thing about a task force was being able to pull from everyone's jurisdiction in order to chase a criminal or make an arrest. A US marshal gave them international networks to draw on. Grayson's FBI background gave them access to the US. And then involving a sheriff, campus police, and Austin PD ensured cooperation and gave them instant local resources.

All of which came in handy when they zeroed in on a perp. It made all the difference in the world when getting close to an arrest of a dangerous criminal and making the charges stick.

Grayson pushed his legs faster. Marshal Remington had outrun him. He could admit he was no Tom Brady despite passing his annual department physical at the top of his age group.

Running wasn't his favorite activity. What he didn't have in speed, he made up for in strength.

Panting, he could only hope the perp had made it out the other end and would make the mistake of running around to the front of the strip mall center, playing into his hands.

Grayson tucked his chin to his chest and pushed his legs harder, pumping his arms to give him the little bit of extra momentum in his sprint.

He wasn't even around the first corner yet. There was

a patch of trees behind the building. The parking lot was cracked from the relentless Texas summers.

They'd received a tip this might be the guy they were looking for and had acted on it fast. As luck would have it, both he and the marshal were within driving distance of the location where the perp was believed to be hiding. Grayson had been farther away than the marshal, so they'd waited for him, keeping an eye on the garage at a distance they'd deemed safe until the deputy walked out in the open in uniform. The perp had caught on and made a run for it.

This perp was going to be slippery. The ones good at killing always were. Otherwise, they would be caught after the first attempt. The general public had no idea how many would-be serial killers out there were caught during the first attempt or immediately after their first murder. It was probably for the best that way. He, for one, knew he didn't want his almost-five-year-old kid walking around scared of the world even though it could be cruel and harsh. It could also be the most amazing place. Grayson had learned those lessons firsthand. The same world that had taken his wife during childbirth had given him a perfectly healthy baby boy.

The world took and the world gave. It wasn't biased. It did the take-give dance with everyone in equal measure.

On the surface, it might seem like some folks got away with gaining and rarely ever had anything taken. But that was a mirage, like water in the middle of the desert. Every person, good or bad, was dealt wins and losses.

Grayson didn't make the rules, because he sure as hell would have done things differently. That was just how it worked. He'd learned the hard way after finding the love of his life in Michelle and then being married only eighteen months before she'd died giving birth to their baby boy, Collin.

She'd named their son, smiled up at Grayson with the most beautiful glow before closing her eyes and bleeding out.

Collin got his mother's sandy-blond hair and blue eyes. He got her bad vision too. Grayson almost chuckled out loud at the thought. Michelle had called herself blind as a bat. She wasn't too far off and had the shin bruises to verify it from being so sure she knew the way to the bathroom without her glasses on when she got up in the middle of the night. The ouches and swear words that would have made his grandmother wash her mouth out with soap as she banged into the end of the bed proved she'd overestimated her abilities.

Then again, that was Michelle. She was always leaping before she looked. Her spontaneous spirit was one of the things he'd loved most about her. The decision to have a baby at all had been spur of the moment. Grayson hadn't thought he would be a good father, based on his own family history.

He'd believed in Michelle's ability to be an amazing mother, though. In the end, that was the reason he'd agreed to go for it.

Collin looked so much like his mother Grayson's heart squeezed every time he looked at his son. His boy had not only inherited his mother's terrible vision but had somehow managed to get her overactive imagination as well.

As he turned the corner, Grayson's blood ran cold. The perp they'd been chasing was at the mouth of the vent where he'd exited and Marshal Remington would come out, and he was hiding behind a trash bin.

# Chapter Two

Pepper spray?

Getting a shot of the fiery liquid right in the face took a second to register. What the hell just happened? Her face burned. The moment of disbelief was immediately followed by the feeling of Abi's eyeballs being wrapped in barbed wire while invisible hands played tug-of-war from opposite sides of her.

Forget about her contacts. They were gone after this. Forget about seeing. Her vision was gone too. She climbed back inside the vent in case the perp decided to take advantage of her weakness.

"Halt!" Agent Chisolm shouted.

Then came the sounds of footsteps, of running.

If not for the FBI agent there would have been a blow to the head coming. Abi was as certain of it as next summer being as brutally hot as this past one.

As if she wasn't in enough discomfort already by the tug-of-war game scratching her eyeballs, the mucus came. Pretty much all the mucus her body could possibly produce came flooding out. The tsunami of tacky syrup flooded every orifice. Trying to see or breathe was punishment.

Now that her mucous membranes were activated and

it felt like a bomb had gone off in her sinuses, her eyes reacted by starting to swell shut.

At this point, all she could do was remind herself life would get a whole lot better in about an hour, when the spray started wearing off. Because feeling like she was swallowing soup every time she tried to breathe was panic-inducing.

The effects might be temporary, but they were hell on wheels while they lasted. Give her a Taser any day of the week over being pepper sprayed. Abi had been misted before during training to be shown what it felt like. Twice in real life. There was no amount of preparation that would get her used to burning corneas or the feeling of choking on thick mucus. Your body wasn't supposed to turn into a weapon against you, but it did when faced with pepper spray.

The sounds of someone's beating feet reminded her the killer was getting away and there wasn't squat she could do about it. There was a patch of woods behind the strip mall. Could he get lost inside? Escape? Could Agent Chisolm catch him? His voice had sounded far away. Was he too far to catch up to the bastard?

This guy had been a fast runner. Then again, a burst of adrenaline could give that extra oomph to reach normally impossible speeds.

Abi forced herself to move to the mouth of the vent where she could listen better to hear if Agent Chisolm was more successful than she'd been.

There wasn't much she could do as she popped out her contacts, one by one, while she could still force her eyelids open. She jammed her fist inside her pants pocket and released the useless pieces of plastic. They were done, so there was no hope of flushing those babies out and popping them back in at some point. There was also no hope of seeing anytime soon either. Everything was a blur.

"Stop or I'll fire," Agent Chisolm warned in the kind of deep, authoritative voice that left no room for argument.

Abi stayed close to the temporary shelter to protect herself while in a vulnerable state. She could no longer hear the perp's footsteps as aggravation settled in. She'd been so close to catching this monster she could almost taste the sweet reward of slapping cuffs on him.

Now?

She was back to square one. Or at the very least, relying on someone else to do the job she should have been able to close.

An engine, a motorcycle engine, revved in the distance. The noise trailed off in the distance a few seconds later. Abi released a string of swear words her grandparents would disapprove of as she listened for Agent Chisolm's footsteps.

"Marshal." His deep timbre, the kind that washed over her and through her like warm, rushing water, broke through her coughing fit.

"Did it have to be pepper spray?" She would almost rather take a bullet in a place she didn't need so much, like nicking her arm or thigh. There'd be a scratch and a little blood but not enough of either to require a hospital stay.

Agent Chisolm's footsteps and heavy breathing alerted her to the fact he was close to her. He wouldn't leave her vulnerable to go after the perp, who must have disappeared in the tree line before hopping on that motorcycle. Plus, it wasn't like he could outrun a bike when he couldn't outrun her.

"Hold on," he said as he called in the motorcycle and

location. "Sheriff has a deputy nearby. Said he would dispatch him immediately."

Abi could only hope the deputy could do what she hadn't...catch the bastard.

"How are you doing?" Agent Chisolm asked.

"I'm good," she lied. It fell into the little lie category. She would be good. That much was truth. And she was willing herself to be good right now.

"You sure about that?" he asked, still panting.

"I'm not planning to drive home if that's what you're asking," she quipped before she could reel it in. They probably hadn't worked together long enough for her to whip out her sarcastic side. Frustration did that to her.

"Good," he said without missing a beat. "I heard you're a horrible driver anyway. The streets will be safer this way."

Abi laughed. She couldn't help herself.

At almost that exact moment, sirens pierced the air. Had the deputy caught the perp?

Abi waited with bated breath. Her pulse kicked up a few notches as minutes passed. A cell phone buzzed. Since hers was back inside her vehicle, it had to be the agent's.

"The deputy can't find him," Grayson said. "He's coming to get more information from us while the sheriff puts out a BOLO in this area."

As she leaned her head against the brick, a sense of failure wrapped long, lean tentacles around Abi.

The sounds of tires spitting gravel came around the back of the building a few minutes after their location had been relayed over the radio.

"Looks like the deputy is here, Marshal Remington."

"If we're going to work together much longer, and from the looks of it we are, I'd rather you call me Abi," she said, hearing the disappointment and frustration in her own voice. Her attitude could get out in front of her. What could she say? As the youngest of three siblings, she'd turned out to be the most spirited. Not unlike the paint horses on her grandparents' ranch. In fact, she'd been compared to the feistier ones more than once.

"Okay, Abi," he said, his voice threatening to crack through her carefully constructed walls—walls that kept everyone out, especially coworkers.

*Her grandparents.* Abi had to force thoughts of them out of her mind so she could maintain focus on the case. As she plopped her backside down on the concrete, she absently fingered the St. Michael pendant they'd given her when she took this job. The sun blaring in her eyes made everything worse.

"He led us here because he had a plan to escape," she said, praying her eyes would stop watering and knowing they were just getting started as her body instinctively rejected the foreign substance. At least all her parts were working, physically speaking. The defense her body launched was top-notch.

"I know," Agent Chisolm agreed. "Call me Grayson if you want me to call you Abi, by the way. Deal?"

She nodded as help arrived a little too late to catch the perp.

Deputy Thad Carlson's voice replaced the once-wailing siren. A car door opened and closed. "I have an unopened bottle of water that might not make the sting go away altogether but it'll help."

"I'd be grateful for anything right now to be honest," Abi said. Truer words had never been spoken.

"Okay," the deputy said. As she heard him approach, a blurry figure came into view. "Tilt your head back."

Normally, Abi would say, *Hell no*, to such a request. The neck was the most vulnerable part of the body. A female wolf will position herself under her mate when threatened just to protect his neck. In this case, Abi would happily make the move if it meant getting some relief from the burning that made her want to literally scratch her eyes out.

The cool liquid spread over her left eye first, followed by her right.

"That's good," she said with a slow exhale. "Amazing, actually." It wasn't as healing as she was letting on, but she wanted to believe it worked so badly she refused to say anything less.

"Hang in there," Deputy Carlson said as he must have emptied the bottle on her face. She'd never known how much skin could burn without having acid thrown on it until she met pepper spray. "The worst of it doesn't last forever."

"Thank the heavens for small miracles," she quipped, once again willing her words to be true.

"Did you, by chance, get a description of the perp?" Deputy Carlson asked.

She shook her head. "Afraid not. Although, since he fit into this vent, we know he can't be as broad-shouldered as Agent Chisolm. He'll be built more like me."

"Taller, though," Grayson added. "And I would have given one to the sheriff when I called him if we'd gotten anything more concrete."

Abi paused, blinking. With her bad eyesight, she wouldn't be able to see well without her contacts anyway. The spray only made her vision marginally worse. At least her eyes weren't swollen completely shut. Still, the effects generally got worse before they improved. Pepper Spray was a long game. "Yes, taller."

"What about you, Agent Chisolm?" Deputy Carlson asked as though Grayson hadn't just made the comment a few seconds ago. Carlson's voice had an air of superiority in it that didn't sit well with Abi. She didn't like having anyone on the task force who believed they were better than anyone else.

"I have nothing to add," Grayson said. "Abi ran a lot faster than I did. By the time I got here, the perp had been waiting at the vent for Abi to come out. He sprayed her and then bolted. I went through the usual steps, gave chase, came up empty."

Deputy Carlson's chuckle fired Abi up. What? Because she was a woman, she couldn't outrun a male counterpart?

GRAYSON SAW ABI'S shoulders bristle at the deputy's slight. She opened her mouth to speak and then clamped it shut again, seeming to think better of whatever comment sat on her lips—lips that he'd noticed had a naturally rose-colored tint. They were full, too. And he didn't need to notice either fact.

"What can I say? Abi should have run track in high school whereas I was more of a power lifter." His urge to defend her honor overtook logic. "Why? Do you have a problem with that?"

"Me? No," Deputy Carlson responded but his tone said otherwise. Was he one of those macho guys whose attitude came from a bygone era? Here was a news flash: women were strong. They were fast runners, sometimes the fastest in the group. He'd seen it play out plenty of times during his years of training and at the gym. Guess what? Some women could out-bench-press all their peers, including men. His Michelle was a case in point. She'd been the smarter one of the two of them: he was one hundred percent certain of the fact. She didn't have an ego that made her want to prove it all the time. Grayson was no slouch. His IQ test had come back top of his class. Of course, he wouldn't have that bragging right if Michelle had been in the room.

A stab of pain pierced him in the middle of the chest. It happened every time he thought about his dead wife. Almost five years had passed, and the pain made it feel like he'd lost her yesterday. Grief was strange, more roller coaster than straight line.

Since the three of them needed to work together and Abi was perfectly capable of taking care of herself, Grayson decided not to split hairs over the deputy's tone. If the guy thought he was winning points with the young and beautiful marshal, he was dead wrong, based on the look on her face.

And, yes, Abi had the kind of looks that people said would stop traffic. Grayson wouldn't disagree. She had the kind of long dark hair with big brown eyes that reminded him of Liv Tyler when she was close to Abi's age, which he believed was twenty-eight years old. Twelve years his junior, but her maturity gave the impression she had a lot more years in law enforcement under her belt.

Grayson hadn't seen instincts like hers in a very long time. But then he'd probably stopped noticing a whole lot of things after losing Michelle within hours of Collin making his appearance in the world.

"I'm guessing you both need a ride," Deputy Carlson offered, unfazed by Abi's physical reaction to his words a few moments ago. Was he unable to read her body language?

Grayson would step in if the deputy crossed a non-negotiable line, like hitting on Abi while on the job. There was a time and a place for everything. Grayson prized his professionalism. Based on what he'd witnessed so far in the short time the task force had been together, Abi held herself to a high standard. Good. They would get along just fine.

Plus, everyone needed to use all their focus to find the bastard who'd gotten away.

"That's correct," Grayson answered as Abi tried to blink her eyes open again. The swelling wouldn't go down for another half hour or so, he knew from experience. Even then, her vision wouldn't return to normal for much longer than that. She was in for a rough ride.

"All right, if the two of you are ready, we can head out now," Deputy Carlson announced. His momentary act of chivalry with the water was overshadowed by his machismo. *Time and place, dude.*

Grayson took a couple of steps toward Abi to close the distance between them, effectively shutting off Deputy Carlson with the move. "Need a hand up?"

She reached for him as she nodded but came up short considering her vision wouldn't return for a while. He found her hand and pulled her to standing with her help.

"My contacts are gone, and I don't keep a spare in my vehicle, not that it would matter today," she said.

"I'll take you to a motel where both of you have been set up by the department for the night," Deputy Carlson said, jumping on the opening.

"I got this," Grayson stated, after asking for keys. "If we're staying at the same motel, it wouldn't make sense for you to go out of your way." He paused, waiting for a retort. When none came, he continued. "Do you mind taking us to my service vehicle near the garage where this all started?" He gave directions to where he'd parked before heading out on foot.

"Will do," Deputy Carlson conceded with the enthusiasm of a little boy who'd just had a piece of candy stripped from his hands.

"I appreciate it," Grayson offered, figuring they needed to maintain a professional relationship.

"What about Marshal Remington's vehicle?" the deputy asked.

"I'll stay with her until she's able to see again and then bring her to retrieve it once she can," Grayson said, solving the problem and leaving no room for alternate ideas. His hunch said Deputy Carlson was looking for an "in" with Abi. Based on her expression, the man would be shot down.

Since Abi didn't give off the impression of being unprofessional, Grayson had no doubt she would be tactful about the rejection. However, she shouldn't have to deal with it after what she'd been through today.

She deserved a "Calgon, Take Me Away" moment like in the commercials his mother used to watch on what felt like repeat.

Deputy Carlson locked in on Abi. "Is that what *you* want?"

"I'm good with whatever," she responded, deflating some of Grayson's bravado. "But it probably makes more sense for Agent Chisolm to take me back to the place we're both staying. It'll save you a trip back and forth when I can see again and can pick up my car."

Deputy Carlson shrugged. "Suit yourself."

Grayson was almost certain he caught a wink from Abi that was aimed in his direction as the deputy puffed up his chest and then turned to walk toward his idling vehicle. Then again, she might have just been trying to blink.

Was he seeing something he wanted to rather than something that was there?

# Chapter Three

"I can't believe he outran and outsmarted me," Abi said to Grayson once they'd been dropped off at his vehicle and Deputy Carlson pulled away after a quick wave. The deputy had said someone would meet them at the motel off the highway with keys. They only had to text a number when they arrived, no need to go to the front desk.

Abi had seen the same dynamic between the deputy and Grayson in other male colleagues. Deputy Carlson had been beating his chest like a silverback gorilla back there, trying to establish dominance.

Having grown up with a brother and two male cousins, she got it. Although she couldn't imagine her family members pulling anything like what she'd just witnessed. To Grayson's credit, he hadn't played along. He'd remained calm and focused while Deputy Carlson tried to one-up him. Seriously, though, did he think she was some kind of prize to be won?

Grayson was a professional. She appreciated him for stepping up to offer assistance, considering she couldn't see for squat right now without her contacts and her eyes still burning like wildfires. Working with a legendary FBI agent like Grayson rattled her nerves more than she wanted to admit. It also made her want to rise to his level and be the best at her job.

Of course, he had more than career achievements working for him. The term *easy on the eyes* came to mind. Along with *superhot* and *hotness on a stick*. He had that whole rugged-mature-gorgeous look down. Don't even get her started on his carved from granite jawline or literal bod of the gods.

"You'll have to be my eyes," she said to Grayson as they stood next to his vehicle. "Who is here and what's going on?"

He provided a quick rundown. The sheriff, accompanied by a pair of deputies, was at the scene of the garage. Activity around the garage said they would be in the way if they stuck around. Plus, her vision was so poor she would only get in the way.

"I keep an overnight bag in my service vehicle along with my handbag," she said, fishing the key fob out of her pocket before clicking it to open the trunk. "Do you mind grabbing them?"

"Not a problem," Grayson said before circling back to her earlier statement and pointing out the perp had a sizable head start or they would be having a different conversation right now.

Right, she forgot to mention just how intelligent Grayson was and how much common sense he possessed. Men who looked like him weren't usually so down-to-earth. There was a sad, almost hollow quality too. An old soul who'd lost someone, maybe. She couldn't quite put her finger on it but still felt a soul-deep connection to it, to him, for reasons she had yet to explain. Since she knew him from work, she would leave the thought there, where it belonged, and walk away, figuratively speaking.

"I'll be right back," he said, leaving the car running as he hopped out to grab her belongings.

Not that she could see him right now, with all the mucus oozing out of her pores.

"That shouldn't have mattered as much as it did," she argued when Grayson returned to the driver's seat. She was still angry the perp was out there, able to kill again.

"We have an escaped victim and a secondary location, which is more than we had to work with before," he said, using more of that practical logic while she was busy beating herself up.

"A witness who was already drunk before being drugged and can't give us a description of the man who spiked his Heineken." Being this close without gaining any useful information was beyond frustrating.

"There were others at the party who might be able to do a better job," Grayson said with a confidence she didn't come close to feeling. "We're figuring out more about the guy's methods. We didn't know he used a secondary location before. The sheriff might find something inside the garage that leads us directly to him. We'll catch him. It's only a matter of time at this point."

"I hope that's true, and I pray it happens before any more lives are lost."

"Agreed," Grayson said. He was a man of few words. She'd noticed how he studied the room a week ago when the task force was first put together.

"I didn't even get close enough to get a good description of the guy, unless you count the back of his head," she continued. The term *beating a dead horse* came to mind on this topic, but she couldn't let it go.

"You outran me," Grayson said. She could hear the slight amusement in his voice.

She could feel her cheeks flush.

"Everyone in law enforcement in the area knows to look out for a male on a motorcycle," he added. "It might not feel like progress yet, but we're moving forward. We've never been this close to the sonofa—"

He caught himself and didn't finish the word, but the same one had been on her mind when it came to this perp.

"What I'm trying to say is don't beat yourself up," he continued. "It's easy to get caught in the trap of always wanting to be perfect. Perfect doesn't arrest criminals any faster. Believe me, I've tried. I've been in your shoes."

"Really? What's different now?" she asked.

"I don't have the energy to waste on being frustrated with myself, so I stopped," he explained. "All my brain power goes to my next move and gleaning any piece of knowledge I can out of what just happened. And we got information. That's successful. Of course, I want to stop someone before any other lives are lost but I can't let emotion cloud my judgment. I'm better at my job when I stay focused. In the long run, fewer people die that way. I have to take the wins as they come."

Those words sounded like they came from hard-knock experience. She could relate on many levels. Abi wasn't just hard on herself for her career moves so she could receive accolades or move up the ladder. She wanted to wrap this case up as quickly as possible for more reasons than the obvious saving lives part. At this very moment, her grandparents were lying in hospital beds fighting for their lives. The folks who'd taken her in and raised her, who'd given her unconditional love, were both in a coma. Where was she?

Not at their sides.

So, yeah, she wanted to wrap this baby up to save the

lives of future victims and so she could request a short leave of absence to go home to Mesa Point. She wouldn't say where she belonged because she'd shaken the dust of that town off her boots and moved a day after graduation. After two years at Austin Community College, she'd transferred to the state's prized school, University of Texas at Austin, to finish her bachelor's degree in criminal justice. She'd worked to put herself through school in a total of three years. She'd casually dated during that time but hadn't found anyone interesting enough to consider having a relationship with.

Here she was now at twenty-eight living her dream job. Her second thought was how empty her townhouse seemed without anyone to share her day with, but that was the frustration mixed with pepper spray talking. Right?

Because right now, thinking about her life, it seemed empty in a way it never had before. She had her sister, brother and cousins. They gave her all the support she needed.

It dawned on her thinking about losing her grandparents was creating a hole in her heart. In her life? Or was it pointing out something she never had?

Abi blinked a few times and gave herself a mental headshake. She was hardcore overthinking her life. Besides, she was getting a chance to work with a legend. Instead of being hard on herself for what she didn't do today, maybe she could pick his brain instead. That sounded a whole lot more productive.

Before she could formulate her first question, he pulled into the parking lot of the motel where they were both staying off the highway. Grayson fired off a text to let the front desk know they'd arrived.

"Are you hungry?" he asked.

"I'd like to circle back and interview the victim, once he's released from the hospital before I think about food," she said.

"How about after we read the sheriff's report, and you can see again?" he asked. "Maybe get some food down. It's lunchtime."

His suggestions were logical. "Okay, then. I could eat," she admitted. At least a half hour had passed since the pepper spray incident. By the time they figured out where to go, secured food and sat somewhere to take it down, she would be mostly clear of the effects. Or at the very least close. "Maybe not right this hot minute but this… party—" she made a sweeping motion around her face, with emphasis on her eyes "—will wear off at some point. Or at the very least become manageable enough to get some food down without choking."

She could have sworn she heard the normally cool and casual agent mumble an apology along with a curse underneath his breath. Was that for not being the one to get there first?

"The guy we're looking for is familiar with the area and mapped out backup plans in case things went south," Grayson finally said after a few moments of silence.

"The motorcycle," she said .

"I think we both know he didn't accidentally find one in those woods," he stated. "He'd stashed it there, possibly when he first came to town."

"The vent had to have been opened or else he knew how to open it fast," she said. "It's not hard to find a party in a small college town. My guess is that he arrived last weekend to check out the scene."

"He could have relatives spread around Texas," Grayson surmised. "They could work at or near colleges."

"The secondary location would make sense if he was trying to hide his activities from them, which obviously he would," Abi pointed out. "The guy didn't miss a beat."

One of the deputies on the scene would stay back to take pictures and dust for prints. Even in an expedited case like this one, it could take weeks to get forensic results. Real law enforcement work wasn't like in the movies or on TV shows. Investigations took time.

In the span of a few weeks, there could easily be two or three new graves. Of course, Reprehensible was "hot" now after leaving a witness and his secondary location. The Mexican government had offered their full cooperation, so that poured on more heat. It was impossible to have agents or officers covering every square inch of university parties, this area, and along both borders. Extra help was always appreciated, especially when they might have to cross a border to make an arrest or follow the criminal.

Under the circumstances, it was highly possible the creep would find another spot to bury his victims, especially after today. But government cooperation was a good place to start.

"The attendant is here with keys," Grayson said as a blurry figure came into view.

"Do you mind if we go inside my room for a few minutes to see if this spray will wear off enough for me to put a fresh pair of contacts in and maybe change clothes?" she asked, thinking she might have a backup pair of glasses in her overnight bag. Abi regretted the question almost the second it left her mouth. The thought of being alone in her room with the handsome FBI agent sent a sensual shiver skittering across her skin. Her body's reaction was every shade of embarrassing.

She'd glanced at the third finger on his left hand at the

first task force meeting. No wedding band, which didn't mean he wasn't married. It just meant he didn't wear a ring. Not uncommon for folks in her line of work, males and females. Some officers preferred to keep their personal life secret. The less a perp figured out, the better.

Was it dangerous to be alone in a motel room with this man?

Abi's heart argued it was and yet she barely knew the agent. Should she listen to emotion or logic? Because her practical mind said she would never be so unprofessional as to fall for someone she worked with. Could she trust it?

GRAYSON CLEARED HIS throat as his cell buzzed. He checked the screen and saw his sitter's number. "Will you excuse me? I need to return a call."

"Yes, of course," Abi said, suddenly looking uncomfortable.

"I'll meet you inside," he reassured after retrieving her bag and purse. He handed them over. "Give me five-ten minutes."

"All right." She reached for the door handle.

"Can you get yourself inside and settled okay?"

"Yeah, sure, no problem," she responded as she felt her way out of the vehicle. She didn't stumble as she walked, which was a good sign she had her balance back. His wife had been half-blind without her glasses, so he could relate to Abi's situation. He didn't want her banging into a door, bruising herself or worse. Once, Michelle had broken a toe on the bedframe. Talk about pain. She'd hopped around the bedroom, in the dark, screaming and holding onto her foot until she crashed into the dresser. Unfortunately, a flat-screen TV sat on that dresser. The bang caused the TV to fall forward, onto her. She knocked it away.

By the time Grayson had turned on the light, the bedroom resembled a junkyard.

Now he could smile at the memory. It hadn't been so funny at the time. Strange how it was the trivial things like that he missed most of all. The way his wife used to sway back and forth to music when she helped him cook. The way she would grab his hand and tug until he relented and danced with her in the kitchen on a random night, dinner be damned.

Michelle made food taste better. She made music sound better. She made the world better.

Now his kid was stuck with one parent. If he had to be trapped with one parent, it should have been his mother. She would know how to handle the bumps and bruises of childhood. She would know how to handle the kids at pre-K who'd made fun of Collin for his glasses. She would know what to bring for the fundraiser bake sales. She certainly wouldn't buy cookies at the store and get busted trying to pass them off as homemade.

Grayson would have traded places with his wife in a heartbeat if it meant his kid got to grow up knowing a woman whose heart was bigger than the Texas sky. Talk about life being unfair. It had dealt a blow to a kid who was only hours old, sticking him with the worst of his two parents.

The only reason Grayson believed he could do the whole "have a kid" at all was because of Michelle. He would have been happy as a lark if they'd limited their family to two, not that he regretted Collin once he was born. But if it had been up to Grayson, his wife would still be alive.

But then, Collin was the best thing that had ever happened to Grayson despite the trials of bringing up a kid on his own and there'd been plenty of those. As a matter of fact, the trials were still racking up.

Grayson's worst fear was that he was doing a terrible job with the kid, who deserved so much better than the dad he got stuck with. Collin was smart for his age. He wasn't athletic in the least. Sports had been Grayson's home turf. He'd made most of his school friends while sweating and battling it out together on the sports field.

Collin's brains came from his mother. She would have known what to do with a brainy, nonathletic kid who had the face of an angel and bottleneck glasses too big for that face. Collin liked to play with figurines or on computer keyboards. Grayson wasn't so sure it was healthy for an almost-five-year-old to stay inside as much as his kid did.

Then again, Grayson didn't have to worry about Collin suffering sports injuries. Unseen benefit?

Despite the challenges and their differences, Grayson couldn't have asked for a better kid. He couldn't love his son more than he did for all those quirks that made him Collin and not a carbon copy of Grayson. He loved his kid for how much he reminded Grayson of Michelle.

He hoped love was enough when it came to bringing up good kids, because it was all Grayson had in his bag of tricks. That and, he hoped, being a good role model.

Grayson called his babysitter. Martha Hope was her name. She was a great aunt to three young adults, with no children of her own. She and Hank, her husband, had taught school together and traveled. He'd taught history and she'd taught math, both working in the same middle school. Martha had lost Hank to a brain tumor six months before Collin was born. Retired, she'd approached Grayson about helping out with Collin a week after they lost

Michelle. Michelle and Martha, as it turned out, had become close while Michelle was stuck on bedrest.

Martha, being an amazing human and great neighbor, needed something to take her mind off losing Hank. She didn't speak the words out loud, but she'd lost Michelle too. All within a brief time period.

Grayson wasn't good with people like his wife had been, but he'd known he was in over his head with a newborn and welcomed the help.

He returned to his vehicle and palmed his cell. Ever since losing Michelle, a dark cloud hung over Grayson's head, and he expected the worst. Every time he got a call from Martha, his chest squeezed like he was waiting for the other shoe to drop.

Taking in a deep breath, he counted backward from five and hit Martha's name on his "missed calls" screen.

Martha answered on the first ring.

"Did something happen to Collin?" Grayson asked, his heart in his throat.

# Chapter Four

Abi managed to step inside motel room number three without face-planting. No small miracle. Since Grayson had asked for privacy with his call, she assumed he was married or in a relationship at the very least. Disappointment stabbed.

When she'd casually glanced at his wedding ring finger first day on the task force, a little spark of excitement had filled her at the realization there was no band and no tan line. Then again, many in law enforcement didn't wear them.

She fell into that camp too. Keeping her personal life private was one of many reasons she didn't do social media outside of work purposes or helping post for the paint horse ranch her grandparents owned and operated since before she was born. *Until now.*

Stubbing her toe on the bedframe, Abi hopped around on one foot in the small space after tossing her bag on top of the bed. Narrowly missing the dresser, she braced herself with a hand on the laminate piece. From here, two steps would get her to the first of two full-size beds and her overnight bag. After losing the perp, she might be on the road again soon.

The couple of steps went off without incident despite

having to hop as her toe screamed in pain from connecting with the frame a few seconds ago. She sat down on the edge of the bed and pulled her overnight bag toward her, cursing the fact they'd anticipated the perp making a move at the nearby university and had been spot-on with their assumption but still hadn't managed to arrest him.

Everyone in the task force had gone in different directions. Spreading out, everyone reasoned, was their best chance to nab the bastard. According to his profile, he was believed to have suffered abuse at the hands of an authority figure. For instance, a mother, father, stepfather, uncle, or possibly a babysitter. In the babysitter scenario, the profiler linked the perp to a college student to explain why he targeted them specifically. Another scenario had the perp in a relationship—male or female since he didn't discriminate based on sex—in which he'd suffered a perceived loss of control or had suffered abuse, be it physical or emotional.

Today reinforced the theory that even though he'd killed five times since the semester began in August, he plotted and planned, making several escape routes before he struck.

Was it even possible to hold a full-time job with this much activity?

Did he target college students for a reason other than possibly having an abusive babysitter who was in college? Or was there another, even simpler reason?

Many young people at that age were looking to party and, therefore, easy prey?

Could it be that simple? Or was there a more sinister explanation?

One thing was certain, the perp targeted a look, which narrowed the suspect list to males and females with brown hair. All five, now six, targets were young students who had been lured away from crowded parties where alcohol was present. Music festivals, frat parties were all fair game for this killer who moved in and around Austin and San Marcos like a ghost. Ketamine had been found in each of his victims' systems. Lab results would be sent out for intended victim number six, who was presently in the ER, but Abi would put money on it coming back positive for the common date-rape drug along with an alcohol content in his blood.

As she fumbled in the bag for her glasses, a couple of knocks sounded before the door cracked open.

"Okay if I come inside?" Grayson asked, his deep timbre sending another round of useless goose bumps up and down her arms. Useless because he was clearly attached. Useless because he was a coworker. Useless because they might never see each other again once this case was over. Abi tried to convince herself it wouldn't matter anyway since she didn't date people she worked with, but the all-knowing voice in the back of her mind laughed. For Grayson, would she make an exception?

"Sure," she said as she slipped on glasses that suddenly embarrassed her. She'd been called all the names on the playground. Four Eyes was the most common and the least appreciated. At least Tommy Gardner had come up with *Cryptoptila immersana* in sixth grade. She'd had to perform an internet search to figure out what he referenced. A moth, as it had turned out, with black dots that looked like eyes running down its back. Tommy got points for originality.

She still felt like a dork without her contacts.

"Nice glasses, by the way," Grayson said after entering.

"Ha ha," she quipped, feeling more self-conscious than she cared to admit.

What she could see of his face twisted. The blurriness was calming down at least. "I happen to like glasses in case you thought that was a joke."

"How's home?" she asked, figuring a change in subject would stave off some of the embarrassment at being wrong. Now that she could see his face more clearly, he'd been serious about the compliment. Why was it easier to believe the opposite was true?

Grayson shot her a warning look. "Good."

"Ready to go?" she asked, figuring they could discuss the case over lunch.

"Did you decide what you wanted to eat?"

Abi shrugged. "My eyes are still burning. Mind if you check to see what our options are? I doubt I could focus on my phone's screen."

Grayson nodded, taking a seat on the end of the bed next to hers. His response to her asking about his home life had caught her off guard. It was normal to keep personal information from perps but they were in a motel room with the door closed. They were coworkers as long as this task force existed. She hadn't expected him to become so defensive about a basic question like the one she'd asked.

Fine, she decided. They didn't need to be chummy on a personal level to be an effective team. Knowing a little about each other could build trust and talking could help pass the time in between the action but Abi reasoned that everyone worked differently. With more years of experience under his belt, Grayson must prefer to stick to the job and then move on once it was over. She wouldn't make the mistake of asking more questions of a personal nature.

Grayson studied his phone. "Tex-Mex, home cooking diner, or tacos?"

"A diner sounds good to me," she said.

"Let's roll."

After locking up the room, which Abi liked, she moved to the passenger side. Grayson surprised her by following her and then opening the door for her.

"Next time, I got it," she said to him before sliding into the leatherette seat of the four-door sedan. At this point, she regretted telling him to call her by her first name instead of Marshal Remington. Abi knew how to keep a relationship professional, dammit.

She folded her arms across her chest and waited for Grayson to claim his seat on the driver's side. Give her another hour or so and she'd be more than ready to be dropped off at her vehicle.

The ride to the diner was spent in silence. It gave Abi time to collect her thoughts.

Grayson parked but didn't get out of the vehicle. "Everything is fine at home. Thanks for asking."

"Okay," she commented before exiting the sedan. What was she supposed to do with that?

Grayson took a minute before following suit. He pocketed his cell phone and keys before saying, "Lead the way inside."

This time, he didn't attempt to open the door to the restaurant. The move meant he'd heard her loud and clear. Abi exhaled slowly. She'd worked with female colleagues who refused to let a male colleague open a door or extend a courtesy. If they were in the heat of a chase, there was no time for those pleasantries, but Abi appreciated the gestures if they were going out for food, which in this case was lunch.

"I overreacted earlier," she said to him as he followed her inside. "If you want to open a door, it's fine with me." Her grandparents' situation had her on edge but that was too personal to explain to someone who'd drawn a clear boundary.

"You reacted to me snapping at you," he said as the hostess greeted them at the stand that was nothing more than a sign that read Please Wait to Be Seated.

"Hello there," the smiling, twentyish blonde said to Grayson. Her gaze barely touched Abi before returning to the gorgeous man standing behind her. "Is it two?"

"Yes," Abi answered for Grayson. The hostess needed to know Abi had a voice too. Grayson's might be deeper and cause an ache to well up from deep inside but that didn't mean he was the only one who could speak for the two of them.

"Okay, then. Follow me." The bubbly hostess in pink hot pants and a polka dotted silk button-down shirt wore a nametag that read Izzy.

Abi did as requested after Izzy grabbed a pair of laminated menus and then led the way. So much for the barcode that had become the norm in recent years. It seemed as though most places had reverted back to handing out hard copies again.

After being seated, she set the menu that had been handed to her down and caught Grayson's gaze. Her thoughts had drifted back to the case on the walk over to the table. "In your professional opinion, how long do you figure we have until he goes for number seven?"

"MY FEAR IS not long and it won't be in this town," Grayson admitted as he glanced around the room. The diner was small and had a cozy feel. It was the kind of place that

Grayson would expect to end up on one of those popular shows that featured diners and drive-ins. Booths lined the walls. The place had an overall everything-pink feel. As long as the food was good, he didn't care what color the vinyl bench seats were. The gravy could be pink for all he cared as long as it tasted the same smothered over chicken fried steak.

This meal, though, he was going for a salad with steak strips. Michelle had always given him a hard time about his diet. Now that he was Collin's primary—and only—parent, he took her advice not to clog his arteries to heart. Literally and figuratively. Before losing his wife, he would have thought nothing of smothering a piece of fried meat with gravy.

He picked up a packet of sugar, flipped it around his fingers. It was a habit he picked up when he focused.

"Mine too," she admitted. "Evidence points to the fact he could strike in a matter of days, but I keep wondering how he'd have time to do the research."

"The guy is a planner," Grayson reasoned. "That might mean he has a master plan behind all of this."

"Certain campuses that he's aiming toward?" Abi compressed her lips and frowned. She did that when she was thinking along the same lines as him. He'd noticed her little tics in the short time they'd been working together. Observing, knowing could mean the different between life and death in a critical moment. Memorizing her habits and facial expressions would tell him when she was in panic mode or in trouble but couldn't say the words outright. Remembering the exact details of her tone would allow him to pick up on nuances that could, once again, mean the difference between action and staying put.

It was all part of the job.

"Exactly my thoughts," Grayson answered after a thoughtful pause.

This place had a retro feel of something that came out of the 1950s. There were vinyl records hung on the walls as decor. The hot pink uniforms and waitresses with their hair tied up in ponytails were also dead giveaways. At this rate, he half expected Richie Cunningham and The Fonz to come waltzing in the front door. And here he'd left his leather jacket at home.

Speaking of home, leaving Collin to go out in the field was getting more and more difficult as his son got older. Kindergarten was on the horizon next year. As much as Grayson hated the idea of becoming a pencil pusher, he had to consider what was best for his family.

The idea of sitting behind a desk made him want to loosen his collar. He was made for the outdoors. One of the many perks of his line of work was travel. Another came in the form of no two days looking the same. But there were dangers too. Grayson could admit that putting his life on the line kept him feeling alive. He'd been stabbed several times, shot twice, and punched more times than he cared to count. His forty-year-old body reminded him that he wasn't in his twenties or thirties anymore. Muscles ached more. Joints hurt when he got out of bed. He was beginning to feel like a football player must after game day.

This, however, was the only job he knew. He'd worked in law enforcement his entire career. As a single parent, though, he couldn't stop the growing feeling that he was being selfish staying with it. He'd thrown out all the usual excuses to keep from changing careers. *People get killed driving their car in traffic every day. No one ever knew when they were going to die. You could get killed walking into the grocery store, or the bank, or a shopping center.* Were they cop-outs because he didn't want to face the truth? He placed his life on the line every time he went after a dangerous felon. Period.

He didn't know when the end would come. But an argument could be made that he was increasing his chances of it coming sooner rather than later.

A desk job waited, and he might as well seriously consider taking it. Once this case was over, he could…

Grayson stopped himself right there. How many times had he seen a "one last case" scenario go south? Too many.

Realizing he'd been lost in thought while working the sugar packet, he lifted his gaze to find Abi studying him.

"Everything okay?" she asked.

"I should be asking you the same question," he deflected.

"All right," she conceded. "I can see now, so that's a plus. Your turn."

Abi was observant and wise beyond her years, assets that would aid her moving up the career ladder. Studying her now, he could perceive there was something going on with her. She'd come highly recommended for the task force, so he doubted it was professional. Personal? Boyfriend trouble? It occurred to him Abi could be married and not wearing a ring. The deputy who'd hit on her back at the strip mall should be embarrassed if that was the case. Hell, he should be embarrassed by his unprofessional actions either way.

A waitress bebopped on over.

The real monster was still on the loose, possibly moving onto his next victim. Could their interview with the latest victim provide a clue as to where the bastard might strike next? Grayson glanced at his cell as the waitress took Abi's order.

A summary from the deputy's interview with the couple who'd been driving the vehicle flagged down by the victim had arrived in his inbox two minutes ago.

The waitress finished up with him, and then promised to put their orders in before heading back toward the kitchen.

"We got something," Grayson said to Abi. Would it be enough to get them back on track before the trail went cold?

# Chapter Five

Abi leaned forward, clasping her hands on top of the table. "I'm listening." The twinge of hope the perp wouldn't get away was premature.

Grayson tapped on his phone's screen. "It's an email with a summary from the couple flagged down by Max Hague."

Her heart went out to the nineteen-year-old whose life would change forever after experiencing a trauma like this one. She recalled several stories, one of which had stuck out in her mind despite not being involved with the case. One of a pair of survivors of Jeffrey Dahmer, who couldn't escape the trauma from nearly being killed at the hands of a monster. He ended up abusing alcohol and drugs. He lived on the streets, unable to work. There'd been multiple arrests for criminal activity. The damage had been life-long. She thought about the story and others a lot. They provided motivation to keep going on the toughest and most dangerous cases. If she could stop one person from suffering, putting her life on the line was worth it.

"The young couple only saw Max Hague running down the street, waving his arms in the air," Grayson supplied. Her chest deflated at the no-news. He rattled off their names and ages, thirty and thirty-two years old. "They almost didn't stop because they thought he was on drugs and might hurt them."

"Does it say why they changed their minds?" she asked.

"The man said he couldn't ignore the desperate pleas for help. He stopped as his girlfriend called 911. The male witness then took off his sweater to give to the naked victim. The female witness helped wrap a picnic blanket around Mr. Hague, who they realized had had bindings on his wrists."

Kind people, she decided. Max Hague might be alive because of them. She'd take whatever luck she could get in this case. "Unfortunately, we already knew this."

Grayson compressed his lips in a frown as he nodded. Abi forced her gaze away from those thick lips of his. What they did was none of her business.

"I wish there was more to the eyewitness account," he conceded. "But that's all we have other than the fact Max Hague was released from the hospital a half hour ago."

"Do we have an address for him?" she continued.

"He's in a dorm on campus," he supplied, then gave the building and room number. That should be easy enough to find.

"Are we authorized to interview the witness?" she asked, not wanting to step on anyone's toes on the task force.

"We need to submit a reason," Grayson said. "I can ask based on the need to verify the profiler's assumptions. That should be enough to get the green light." He fired off an email.

Abi was already on tentative ground with the deputy after she had rebutted his advances, and Grayson's position was worse after their exchange. One person working against them on the task force wasn't the end of the world. Carlson shouldn't be enough to hold them back.

Abi's turkey burger and sweet potato fries arrived along with Grayson's steak salad.

She picked hers up as he finished typing the request. "Looks like a heart-stopping meal you've got there."

"This?" Grayson asked, switching gears with a smile. "I'm as healthy as a horse."

She shot him a look before taking a bite of her turkey burger.

"What?"

"Nothing," she responded after chewing. At least they could kill time by eating while they waited for the go-ahead to interview the witness. Working with a task force had its disadvantages and benefits. Multiple interviews with a victim could traumatize the person further, so most of the time teams did their best to minimize the number. For Abi, she excelled at witness interviews, so it was difficult to trust anyone else's.

"Do you have a problem with me saying I'm as healthy as a horse?" he asked after a bite of salad. He motioned to his plate as if to say, *Case in point*.

"What do you know about horses?" she asked. The subject gave her mixed feelings. One the one hand, she'd loved growing up on a horse ranch. But she couldn't think of them without her mind snapping to the picture of her beloved grandparents in the hospital fighting for their lives.

"Not much, to be honest," he said.

"I could tell," she quipped, trying to shake the sadness that came with thinking about them.

"How is that?" he continued.

Giving up a few details of her background wouldn't exactly qualify as getting personal. "I grew up on a paint horse ranch."

"I didn't know that," Grayson said.

"Why would you?" She cocked an eyebrow at him as she tossed a fry in her mouth. The food here wouldn't make up for the awful day she'd been having so far but at least she was able to get a quality meal. It was small, but something. In the worst of situations, Abi tried to find one positive thing to focus on if only for a few moments. When it came to her grandparents, though, she couldn't. Their lives were in limbo. Waking from their comas was not guaranteed.

Grayson shrugged. "Good point. I guess we don't know much about each other's backgrounds."

"No need to," she qualified.

"What was it like?" he continued. "Growing up on a horse ranch. I imagine it's every little kid's dream."

She involuntary shivered at the word *kid*.

Grayson cleared his throat. A look flashed behind his eyes that she couldn't quite pinpoint. What did he care if she didn't like kids?

"It's as great as everyone assumes it would be," she conceded, biting down on her bottom lip after returning to the original conversation. "I loved every minute of being outside with the horses, learning how to break them so they could be sold. I loved exercising them." Moisture gathered in her eyes at the memories, catching her off guard. Abi turned to face the wall before sniffing tears back. "Sorry."

He set a couple of napkins on her side of the table. "I've seen tears before, Abi. It's not a big deal."

"It's probably just leftover pepper spray," she insisted. "My tear ducts are overreacting." She took the napkins and patted the corners of her eyes underneath her glasses. "I'm good."

"Like I said before, I like those glasses on you better than contacts," Grayson said after another bite of food.

"Yeah, funny," she said. Now he was just being nice out of sympathy.

"I mean it." He set down his fork and studied her. "The color of the frames compliments your eyes."

"Oh," she said, realizing he actually meant those words. "Thank you."

"And you're probably right about the pepper spray still reacting."

Now he really was just being kind. Either way, she would take the out. Crying while on the job wasn't something she'd ever done before and had no plans to do again. Emotion had been building since hearing the news back home and she'd been holding everything in. It shouldn't be a surprise some of it found a way to leak out.

They finished their meals and paid the bill. Abi managed to make it through the rest of her turkey burger without another wet droplet from her eyes. She did, however, make a mental note to call her sister later this evening for an update. Crystal had taken leave from work to hold vigil at the hospital. It would be Abi's turn next. Their brother, Duke, had taken the first round.

Grayson's cell phone dinged as they returned to his vehicle. "We got permission to interview the victim."

Abi put her worries about her grandparents aside. Right now, all her focus had to be on interviewing Max Hague.

GRAYSON TOOK THE driver's seat after opening Abi's door for her. This time, she thanked him and smiled, lighting a half a dozen campfires inside him. They drove to the small campus of West Texas College and to the dorm parking lot aptly named Residence Hall. There was no miss-

ing the three-story redbrick building, considering it was
the only dorm on campus according to the map Abi had
pulled up on her phone on the way over. Easy enough.

They walked to the Hall and stood at the glass-and-
metal door where a security pad was mounted on the red
bricks. A pair of male students came walking out almost
immediately, so Abi, who might be perceived as the less
threatening of the two of them, grabbed the door before
it closed again. She smiled at the pair of young students.
They nodded while keeping their conversation going.
Something about a hard test and a professor who pulled
questions from the test bank.

Grayson held the door open. "After you."

Abi walked in first and quickly located an elevator.
The traditional building was on the newer side. Inside,
the tile floors were scuffed and there were mud tracks
from recent rain. A pegboard with pins held announce-
ments and advertisements.

"What's the number?" Abi asked after pushing the up
button.

"Two-twenty-one," he supplied.

Abi pushed the number two once inside. They probably could have walked up the stairs, but the elevator was
closer. Metal doors closed and the elevator surged. Abi
reached for Grayson to steady herself, grabbing a fistful
of his shirt in the process.

"Whoa!" she said.

A ding sounded and the elevator jolted to a stop.

"Remind me to take the stairs back down," she said as
the doors opened again.

Grayson cracked a smile. "One flight doesn't seem so
bad compared to that antiquated metal box."

"No, it doesn't," she agreed before straightening her

shirt and flicking lint from her pants. Even disheveled, she would look amazing.

Grayson wiped the smile from his face as they approached Max's room. A flurry of voices sounded on the other side of the door.

Abi took a deep breath, glanced over at him, and seemed to get the response she wanted, because she knocked twice before opening the door.

Two young men met them at the door, blocking the view inside. The Asian man was tall and had the build of a football player. The Caucasian male next to him was a full head shorter and much thinner but filled the rest of the doorframe. He looked like what most folks decided a gamer should—skinny with glasses and not a lot of muscle. That was the general stereotype Grayson came across. He could see over the young man's head.

"Can we help you?" Football guy asked, sizing them both up.

"My name is Marshal Abi Remington," Abi started, her voice soft enough to recite a lullaby. She produced her badge from the belt holding up her slacks. "My partner Agent Chisolm and I have a few questions for Max Hague." In a classy move, she maintained eye contact with the Football guy rather than crane her neck to see if Max was hiding in the room. "Is he here?"

"Yes, ma'am," Football guy said without budging. He turned his head to one side and then asked, "Are you up to talking to anyone, Max?"

"Okay," came the unsteady voice.

"Mind if we stay?" Football guy asked.

"If it will make everyone more comfortable," Abi conceded. Her gracefulness with victims was up there with the best Grayson had ever witnessed.

Football guy stepped aside and then took a seat on the bunk across from Max's. Gamer guy followed suit as though a shadow, giving a view to Max who was seated on the floor. Grayson had to hand it to the young men: they were ready to stand up and defend their friend from unwanted guests. He had a lot of respect for that.

"We're sorry to intrude," Abi said calmly to Max.

"My parents are on their way from El Paso," Max stated as he stuffed a trunk with books and laundry that he picked up piece by piece on the floor and shoved inside. "I'm leaving school. Finishing the rest of the semester remotely." He barely glanced at Abi and Grayson as they stood just inside the door.

Abi's shoulders were relaxed as she leaned against the frame. She tented her fingers together, indicating she was the one in charge in the room.

Max wasn't taller than five feet seven inches. He wore baggy sweatpants and an oversize hoodie. His brown eyes were wild when he focused on Abi. "I can't stay here anymore after what…"

"You've been through a traumatic experience," Abi said with the kind of compassion that made Max stop long enough to move to his bed and then plop down. He tilted his face toward the ceiling as he closed his eyes and took in a deep breath.

"We're here to help you, Max. Going through the details of what happened isn't going to be easy," Abi said. As she crossed the room, one of Max's friends stood up. No doubt, he would place himself between her and Max. Abi put a hand out to stop the young man from intervening, and in a surprise move, he froze. "But it will be worth it once we stop this monster." She paused, letting those words sink in. "Can you help us, Max?"

Max opened his eyes the second she got within five feet of him. Abi slowed, making eye contact the whole time. She had a gentle, calming tone like the one he imagined a horse whisperer would use. Growing up on a horse ranch might have honed those skills.

She crouched down in front of Max when she made it to within a foot of him. The nonthreatening position allowed Max to feel in charge. "There's a very bad man out there, Max. I know it. You know it. My partner and I want to stop him before he moves on to the next victim."

Max started to open up but then clamped his mouth shut. Young people were usually afraid to talk when they'd done something wrong in the process.

"I'm not here to give you a hard time about underage drinking." Her soft but determined tone resonated with Max. "All I'm after is the truth about what happened so this horrible person can be stopped. Any information you can provide will help. I promise."

Max nodded as he gathered courage. His gaze flicked over her head, to his friends.

"I can ask them to leave the room if that makes it easier for you to talk about it," Abi said, her voice as soothing as honey on a sore throat.

"Yeah, man, we can wait in the hallway if you want," Football guy offered. "Either way, bro."

Max gave a tentative nod.

"We'll be right outside that door," Football guy said as he and the other friend stood.

"Promise you won't leave?" Max's voice was small and vulnerable.

"I'm not going anywhere, man."

"We can keep the door open if that helps," Abi offered, keeping her compassionate gaze steady on Max.

"Okay," Max said before the pair exited into the hallway.

Grayson might have been in this business longer than Abi, but he was witnessing a master at work. Her special touch had Max's shoulders relaxing and his breathing almost back to normal. It wasn't uncommon for a victim's heart to race when law enforcement arrived even though they weren't guilty of anything. The stress of the event flooded them, and in many cases involving young people, they worried they'd done something wrong.

Once the others were gone, Abi sat down on the floor, crisscrossing her legs.

"Start whenever you're ready," she said to Max.

# Chapter Six

Max Hague took in a deep breath. He exhaled slowly, brought up his right foot to rest his ankle on his left thigh. He clasped his hands around his right knee as it shook. "My parents don't know about me." His gaze shot from Abi to Grayson and back. "About my lifestyle."

"We have no judgment on how you live your life and no reason to discuss your lifestyle with your parents," Abi reassured. "You are a college student. The rest is up to you to tell them when and if you're ever ready." Half the battle in getting good information from a victim was making them comfortable in your presence. It was the reason she sat on the floor while Max stayed on the edge of the bed. He'd been victimized, almost killed. He felt helpless. Having him sit taller than Abi gave some of his power back. It was a psychological trick she'd picked up early in her career from working with several young victims about to go into the WITSEC program. Plus, her heart really did go out to Max. The kid would likely have trust issues for years to come, if not the rest of his life.

Abi might have an aversion to kids, but she didn't mind teenagers. Most people thought she had it flipped. Except that she had no idea what to do with a crying baby or a toddler in the middle of a temper tantrum. They looked demon-possessed and scared the bejesus out of her. By fifteen years old, though, they had opinions of their own. She'd had lively conversations with teenagers. Plus, they could go to the bathroom on their own and wipe their own backsides. No need to change any stinky diapers. So that was a huge plus.

Max gave another tentative nod. "I don't remember much."

The brain often blocked out details of a traumatic event, not to mention the effects of ketamine.

"Anything you can give us will be helpful," she continued. Grayson took to the background on this one, letting her take the lead. In this case, it was best. Logic said he would most likely be more suspicious of men. A woman's presence, however, could have the opposite effect. Grayson didn't seem to mind playing the odds on this one and the strategy seemed to be working. On a human side, she didn't want to inflict more pain on a victim. They deserved to be treated with compassion, which clearly was her strength.

Max kept his eyes closed as Abi told him to start from the beginning and take his time with the details.

"It's hazy," Max said. "One minute, I'm at a party having a great time, dancing and talking with friends. The next, I'm in someone's car." He paused. "The next thing I know, I'm in the back seat. Someone is on top of me, holding me down." His bottom lip quivered.

"It's okay," Abi soothed. "You're doing great, and we can stop at any time if you need a break."

Max closed his eyes and gave a slight nod.

"What do you remember about that moment?" Abi asked.

"The feel of plastic gloves against my skin, like at the

doctor's," he said before opening his eyes. "I didn't remember that before, but he had on gloves like he was going into surgery or something. Purple. They were purple."

"Can you recall what else he wore?" she asked, wondering if the car part was true or if he'd confused it for the garage. Then again, there could be a bench seat in the garage. She would have to read the sheriff's report once it was sent to the group.

Max shook his head. "I already told the deputy who visited me at the hospital this part is fuzzy." The date rape drug would cloud his memory. It was one of the reasons that ketamine or similar drugs were so popular aside from the ease of slipping them inside someone's drink. "All I know is the person was strong." It could have been the drug that had made Max compliant, more than the perp's arm strength. Perception was skewed with those drugs. Then again, the perp had to be somewhat strong in order to handle his victims.

"Would you say he was tall? Heavy?" she asked.

"Tall, I think," Max said. "When you're my height, it's not hard to beat."

"Heavy?"

"I don't know," Max said on a sharp sigh. "The clothes he had on were loose, baggy. Made it impossible to tell."

"In the back seat of the vehicle, were you facing up, to the side, or down?" she asked.

"Down."

"And then what happened?" she continued.

"The pressure on me ended, and then I was told to strip off my clothes," he said with an involuntary shiver at the memory. "I did what he said. Then the guy disappeared for a little while. Or I passed out. I'd been drinking all night, so…" The perp must have wanted to strip Max to make it more difficult for him to run, or more scared to make a wrong move.

"Did he threaten you?" she asked.

"Said he would kill me if I didn't listen." Max nodded as he rubbed his wrists. "He put some kind of restraints on my wrists, though. But honestly, I don't remember much of that. I just noticed it after I ran."

Face down on whatever seat was in the garage, arms tied presumably behind his back, Max would be easier to subdue. Sadly, Reprehensible's other vics had marks on their wrists too. The forensic report on the first vic had confirmed some type of plastic was used. A zip tie came to mind. They could be purchased at hardware stores or any of those big-box DIY places.

"Do you have a guess as to what kind of material was used?" she asked but she could read the report to find the answer. This was a way to check facts. She didn't believe Max would lie about his experience. He had no reason to. His answers would tell her how lucid he'd been and how reliable the information might be.

"No," Max admitted. "All I know is it cut into my wrists." He held them out for inspection. They resembled burn marks. Abi scooted closer, careful not to invade his personal space. The red marks could have come from a zip tie or rope. They were probably too thin for rope burns, though. Could be plastic or wire, based on the cuts. If plastic had been confirmed on vic number one, she would put money on the perp using the same material here too.

"Before the vehicle, can you tell me anything you remember from the party?" she asked, hoping to backtrack.

"Not really," Max said. "It was in someone's backyard." He flashed eyes at her. "We were drinking and there was music, the usual stuff. The neighbors were there, so no one was worried about the cops being called." He seemed to catch himself as guilt flashed over his features. He was telling someone in law enforcement that he'd broken the law with underage drinking. "People were partying, you know, so mingling and dancing."

"Did you stay outside the entire time or go into the house?" she asked.

"Yeah, we were all banned from using the house," he said, looking up and to the right, a sign of recall. "No one was allowed inside after the last party when Micky dropped a bottle of tequila in the living room. Aiden said the place still reeked. We couldn't even use the bathroom. He told us to go behind the bushes." It was possible Max had been watched.

"What about recreational drugs?" Abi asked but Max was already shaking his head.

"I don't do those," he said emphatically. Could she believe him? Admitting to drinking had been difficult enough. Alcohol was legal for those old enough to consume it. Drugs were a different ball game. "I would never take anything. All I do is drink on the weekends." His demeanor changed and guilt flashed across his features, which probably meant he'd experimented at the very least. But he wasn't willing to own up to it and she wouldn't know for certain until toxicology reports came back. A drug screening panel would have been run in the hospital, but those didn't cover all drugs, just the main culprits.

"What about pictures?" she asked. "Social media?"

"I mean someone always pulls out their phone to take pictures, but we have a rule about nothing being posted on social," Max said. "It's an easy way to get kicked out of the university since there's a hard rule against underage drinking."

The sheriff had already requested partygoers come in voluntarily and bring their phones. She had no idea how many young people would take him up on the request. Many would guard their pictures with their lives if they thought someone would get into trouble with the law. A few would come forward, though. Some people would do the right thing after news got out. On a small campus, it wouldn't take long for word to spread.

"Did you ever lose track of your drink at any point in the party?" Abi continued.

"No, I…well, actually, there was an outdoor bar near the back fence. I may have set it down a few times while grooving," he admitted. "I didn't remember that before either. Now that I think about it, though, I'm sure I set my cup down multiple times to dance. Or even just to talk to someone."

Women were warned about date rape drugs and told how to protect themselves. Information was out there for everyone. However, she wondered how many guys actually paid attention to flyers or warning ads, thinking it would never happen to them.

"Anyone at the party could have had access to your cup, then," she said. She and Grayson could get the house resident's full name and the address easily enough from the report. She already had the names Micky and Aiden. She wouldn't dig deeper into those questions with Max when the information would be readily available in the report.

"I'm afraid so," he said after he thought about it for a few seconds. It was obvious from the dilation of his eyes that he was still in at least a mild state of shock. The drug he'd been given last night would have lingering effects. It had only been fifteen hours, give or take. Not to mention the massive hangover from all the drinking. But he mostly came across as frightened of his own shadow. There was a bandage over a cotton pad on the inside of his left arm. The hospital would have taken blood for testing and most likely rehydrated him with an IV. "We all drank out of those red Solo cups. I'm pretty sure I picked up the wrong one after getting a mouthful of tequila at one point. Someone was drinking it straight up with no mixer." Max's face twisted. Then he shook his head. "I get sick off anything but beer."

Abi didn't want to think about the hangover that a drink such as straight tequila in a Solo cup would bring on. And that was after possibly throwing up. College kids and binge drinking seemed to go hand in hand. She realized that didn't apply to all college students, just to note that it was still common when young people got their freedom for the first time.

It also sounded like someone else might have been the target, except that Max fit the physical description of Reprehensible's prior victims.

"I'm sure you gave the deputy a list of names of the attendees at the party," Abi said.

"I did," Max stated.

She wouldn't trouble him twice since the list would be in the deputy's report—a report he was most likely putting together right now.

From roughly 1:30 in the morning to 7:30 a.m. when Max flagged down the couple, Reprehensible could have done anything he wanted. Max was compliant due to the drugs in his system.

"Was it a big party?" she asked.

Max nodded. "Could have easily been a hundred people or more in the couple of hours I was there. It's not unusual to hop from party to party."

There weren't enough resources to interview every individual.

"How frequent are the parties?" she asked, wondering if the same core group traveled from place to place. If she could narrow the number down, it would be worthwhile to interview a handful of young people. Then again, waste too much time here and Reynosa might already be on to his next vic.

"There's something going on every weekend," Max said, dropping his leg, stretching both and crossing them at the ankles. "At least, usually. Plus, there's not much else to do in a small town except get-togethers." His hand trembled as he bit his thumbnail.

"I know you've been asked this question multiple times but is there anything else you remember about the person who did this to you?" Abi asked.

Max sat quiet for a long moment. "His voice sounded like he was talking through a fan. You know how that sounds. Like it's some kind of effect."

The perp didn't want anyone to be able to pinpoint him from his voice, she noted. Having a living witness made her wonder if the perp would try to circle back and murder Max. His parents must be thinking along the same lines, which could be one of the reasons they were pulling him from school. That, and the fact he'd just been through a horribly traumatic event and needed time to recover.

"Oh," Max said, brightening up. "I think he has a mole on his neck. It was dark. Big."

"I thought it was dark outside and he was clothed to the hilt," Abi said.

"It was and he was," Max confirmed. "But I remember a flash of light and then seeing it." He frowned. "At least, I think so." His shoulders deflated before he straightened up and stood. "I could be confusing memories, mixing them up. I've been woozy ever since it happened. The brain fog is real. At the time, it felt like I was going in and out of a dream. None of it felt real. It still doesn't."

"I understand," was all Abi could say. They had something more…a neck mole.

But not much else.

"Does anything else stand out in your mind that you might have forgotten to mention earlier?" she asked.

He sat there for a long moment. At nineteen, he was part adult, part child. His current expression was all kid.

"Thank you for your time, Max," she said, figuring this conversation was over. He'd already stood up and returned to packing.

"You're welcome," he said, his hand still trembling. "Will you tell the guys they can come back in?"

On the way out, she did just that after providing her contact information to Max and asking if he'd be more comfortable if they waited around until his parents arrived before taking off. He gave them the okay to go since his buddies were nearby. Abi was relieved Max had such devoted friends. He would need them in the coming days and weeks. If he was to have any chance of recovering from the psychological effects of a crime like the one he'd survived, he would need a strong support network from here on out.

"GOOD JOB IN THERE," Grayson said once they reached the elevators. The doors opened. An older couple came rushing out. The panicked look on the older woman's face said she was Max's mother. His father, an older version of Max, was so distracted that he ran into Grayson's chest.

"Sorry," the senior Max said before rushing down the hallway in the direction of his son's room.

A knot tightened in Grayson's chest as they walked to the stairs. His mind immediately snapped to his little boy, who was presently home with a babysitter instead of a parent.

An almost debilitating wave of guilt stabbed Grayson in the center of the chest at the thought of letting Michelle down, his son down. During their eighteen-month marriage, they'd never once talked about the possibility of him not coming home from work. Two years of dating beforehand, they hadn't broached the subject. Michelle knew his job was dangerous. She'd been fully aware of the risks while they were dating. Both had been superstitious about bringing up the subject, though. They'd agreed not to discuss what could go wrong in life, talking around the topic. Instead, they'd focused on what could go right. At least, Michelle had. Her belief in him knew no bounds. Coming home to her had made him want to be a better person.

The thought of his wife being the one to die had been unimaginable. She'd given up her career as a wedding photographer after Collin's birth to stay home with him full-time. Michelle had wanted at least two kids. Grayson had countered they should see if they were any good with one.

He would have given her anything she wanted.

After heading down one flight, they exited the building.

"Hey," Abi said, her voice breaking through his reverie.

Grayson cleared his throat in an attempt to dislodge the emotion stuck there. "Good interview, by the way."

"Thanks, but you already said that," she said, confusion in her voice.

He needed to steer the conversation to the case before she could ask him where he'd gone just now. He'd accepted the fact his wife was gone. Revisiting their past only came about when he thought about the disservice he was doing to her by not being home for Collin. Then again, they'd had no contingency plan. They'd never spoken about what her wishes would be if—heaven forbid—one of them died before their son reached his eighteenth birthday, let alone after his birth. Since Michelle was gone, Grayson needed to figure it out on his own. In addition to Abi's other good qualities, she was kind and intelligent. She knew when to push and when to pull back.

He shook off the temptation to talk about his personal life with a coworker. *Temporary coworker,* that same voice pointed out.

"What are your takeaways after speaking to Max directly?" he asked, getting the conversation back to the case.

"That he is still in shock and trying to process," she said. "We didn't get as much as I would have liked."

"The possible mole is interesting," he pointed out.

"Thanks," Abi said. "True about the mole, except his brain is so jumbled. Plus, with alcohol consumption, he admitted to not knowing if he could trust what he was saying, let alone us use it to move forward."

"All good information for the report," he said. It was something. Progress might be a game of inches right now, but he believed he could find more clues.

They didn't have time to discuss their personal lives. Although, after seeing her way with Max, Grayson wondered if he could bounce a few ideas off her as a friend instead of coworker. Friends had been in short supply lately. And they wouldn't be coworkers for long.

Could he forge a friendship with Abi?

# Chapter Seven

"I thought about making a short list of young people who visited the parties regularly, but the deputy most likely did that," Grayson said to Abi after reclaiming the driver's seat. She leaned back in the seat and pinched the bridge of her nose. A raging headache threatened. It was late. She wanted a warm shower and a comfortable bed.

"Same here," she said, sitting up a little straighter. "I need to go back to my room and make a supplemental victim interview report. Do you want to join me? We could wait for the other reports to be uploaded. Go over them together."

"It couldn't hurt to go over the details of the deputy's summary," he agreed. Her heart gave a little flip at spending more time together. Abi reminded herself being in the same room would benefit the case. Two heads were better than one. Plus, Grayson was a seasoned agent. She wouldn't mind picking his brain.

Also, by now, reports might be uploaded. They could stay in and order pizza for dinner while they broke everything down. Once they had names and addresses, they could go out together to interview witnesses. She also wanted to go to the scene of the party at night to see how easy it would be to watch the backyard activities.

"He's moved on," she said, tapping her forehead, trying to distract herself from the dull ache. Ibuprofen only lasted so long and hers had run out. At least for tonight, they would be better served going over the information.

"I know," Grayson responded. "There's no way he would stick around here after almost getting caught. I'm assuming he's already ditched the motorcycle by now too. It might have been stolen. Or at the very least he might have switched the plates so it couldn't be traced back to him."

"Right. Makes sense." She paused. "Based on your years of experience, how long do you think we have before he strikes again?" The part of her that wanted to rest didn't want to know the answer to that question. Because she knew in her bones it would be soon. Too soon. The effects of the pepper spray might have worn off but that didn't mean she wasn't worn out. Today had been one for the books and it was still going. She glanced at the clock on the dashboard: 5:55. Some people saw it as a good omen when you looked at a clock and all the numbers matched. She would take whatever luck she could get in this case.

"We got close to catching him this time," Grayson said. "While most serial killers would wait, I believe this one will strike soon because it's the last thing we'd expect."

"Logic says pull back and make certain the coast is clear," she said.

"His pattern has been cutting the time in between kills rather than the other way around," he said. "He's not regrouping after he strikes…"

"He's moving on to the next," she said. "Considering the time in between kills shortens, he mapped this out beforehand."

"Not the individuals, though," Grayson said. "Those, I believe at least, he takes at an opportune time."

"It would be easy enough to have locations scouted, even parties. They occur on a regular basis on and around college campuses." Repeating those last words as she'd done many times during this case wasn't providing the breakthrough she'd been hoping for. Sometimes, repetition helped. Not today. The headache was making it more difficult to concentrate too. A shower and fresh, clean clothes might wake her up. If not, she could down a shot of espresso. Or whatever coffee the motel stocked. "I need more ibuprofen if I'm going to use my brain much more."

"He'll strike soon, but not tonight," Grayson predicted. "If you want to write and submit the report, we can always swing back by the house for a quick look after dinner. Then, start fresh early in the morning."

"As much as I hate to admit it, that might not be a bad idea," she said. "Sometimes, when I'm too focused on a case, the answers move further away. Maybe we should talk about something else for the rest of the ride back."

"Your cousin Julie has been getting word out to every college in Texas to make sure faculty and students are aware of the situation," Grayson said. Abi's cousin was also a US marshal. "That's as much as can be done anyway."

"I know you don't discuss your personal life—"

"Any chance you'll let me edit that statement?" he interrupted.

"Depends on the edit," she said, turning to look at him. Abi considered herself good at reading people. Grayson had definitely just stepped out of his comfort zone.

"I don't normally discuss my personal life with coworkers but I'm not against gaining a new friend," he said. "What do you think?"

Abi wasn't sure what changed his mind, but she liked Grayson. He was honest and genuine. She could easily shelve the unwanted attraction she felt toward him. Maybe not *easily*. But she could set it aside, ignore it. "I'm good with being friends." She could use one considering everything going on at the ranch while she was on this case.

"What's your opinion about kids?" he asked.

"Not for me," she said. "But I guess they're fine for other people."

"You don't want to have children?" His question was loaded with shock. Enough to catch her off guard. Was he one of those people who thought every woman wanted 2.5 kids and a white picket fence?

"I don't like them enough to want to have one," she quipped.

Grayson laughed.

"What? I'm supposed to want them because I have ovaries?" she asked, more than a little indignant.

"No, it's not that," he said. "I was looking for advice but you're not the right person to ask."

"*You* want to have kids?" she asked, confused.

"No," he corrected. "I *have* a kid. The call I took earlier was from my babysitter."

"Wouldn't you want to talk to your wife about your kid?" Abi asked.

"That's the rub," he said with the kind of sadness in his voice that said he'd been through something terrible. "She died almost five years ago."

"I'm so sorry, Grayson," she said and meant every word. "I had no idea. That must have been awful."

"It was, but I've had time to get used to it," he said.

"Five years is a long time. I appreciate your sympathy, though."

"Of course," she stated. "How old is your kid?"

"Almost five years old."

"Oh." Abi didn't know what to say, so she reached over and touched his forearm.

"It happened during childbirth," he continued.

Her heart went out to the man. She couldn't imagine finding the love of her life and then losing them so quickly. And immediately after starting a family.

"I used to have the same reaction about having kids as you just did," he said.

"What changed your mind?"

"Michelle," he said. "That was her name."

"It's a lovely name," Abi said.

"Thank you." He paused for a few moments. Was he catching his breath? "She was confident I'd be a good father."

"But you weren't," Abi surmised.

"Not in the least," he admitted.

Losing the person you loved most in the world would put the haunted look in his eyes. She'd never spent time with anyone who made her think about having a future together but if she had, she would have wanted it to be someone like Grayson. She would have wanted it to be with someone who loved her like he must have loved Michelle.

She also realized that anyone else he might be in a relationship with in the future would be competing with a ghost.

ABI HAD A way with people. Her words soothed him in places that had been encased in a hard shell for almost five years now. It was the reason he could keep going. "This job is dangerous."

"True," she said, cocking her head to one side. "But we knew that when we signed up, right?"

"That was before I was a single parent," he pointed out.

"What's changed?" she asked. "You've been on your own for quite a few years now. I assume everything has been going well."

"Collin is about to go into kindergarten," Grayson continued.

"And so?"

"He's starting school next year," he said. "Who will help him with his homework every night?"

"I don't know much about kids to be perfectly honest, but I don't remember having a whole lot of homework in kindergarten," she said. "I'm pretty sure we sang a lot of songs, held hands and played tag on the playground."

"He needs stability," he said.

"How are you not providing that?" she asked. "You have a job that requires you to be away. No different than a businessman who travels for work. Don't you agree?"

"Well, yeah, but last time I checked businessmen didn't have bullets flying past their heads."

"Good point," she admitted. "But doesn't working in your dream job make you a better parent? Doesn't it teach your kid to be happy and do the kind of work you love?"

He didn't immediately speak. He'd loved his job at one time. Did he still?

"When you love it, that's true," he said as he drove past the crime scene on the way to the motel.

At the four-way stop, he glanced over at Abi, who nodded her head and pursed her lips. "My grandfather was a US marshal a long time ago."

"I thought you said he owned a horse ranch or is this your grandfather on the other side of the family?"

"Same one," she reassured. "He worked the job when he was young but got burned out on it after a few years. He didn't like being away from my grandmother so much."

Grayson felt that statement in his bones about being away from Collin.

"He squirreled away every penny to scrape up enough money to buy land and then fix up the home there," she said with a wistful quality to her tone as she turned her face away from him, toward the passenger window.

Did he hear her sniffle?

"I'm guessing he left his job after building his horse business," he said. Being outside sounded damn good to Grayson right now. Being on the land. Watching the sunrise in the mornings with a cup of coffee in his hand. Collin having room to run around a big yard. Grayson dialed back his enthusiasm. Not only was his kid not athletic but he was allergic to grass. Grass and almost everything else in the environment too.

"That's right," she confirmed. Then came the sniff before she took in a deep breath.

"Doesn't sound like a bad life to me," Grayson admitted.

"Is that what you want?"

"I'm qualified to sit behind a desk for the rest of my career," he said. "Which sounds like hell to me." Then he turned the tables. "Have you ever wanted to do anything else other than work for the Marshals Service?"

"Wanted to be a cowgirl on the rodeo circuit when I was eight," she said with a laugh that was almost musical. "Does that count?"

"Only if by age ten you wanted to be a vet," he retorted.

"Most definitely," she said. "I can tell you one thing. I was never one of those girls who sat around and played with dolls or dressed up in high heels or experimented with makeup. Those things never appealed to me when I was young."

"You were busy living most kids' dream of growing up on a horse ranch," he interjected.

"Well, that's true enough. I was mucking stalls in overalls before school two mornings a week," she said.

"Lucky kids who got to sit next to you in class," he quipped.

Abi laughed. The break in tension was good. Talking about his personal life had never appealed to him before. Was he missing having friends? Rather than hit happy hour after office work or after shooting range practice, he headed home to Collin. During the time he wasn't in the field, the least he could do was be home for his kid. So he didn't date. At least, not traditionally. While Collin was in preschool, Grayson had gone out to a few lunches here and there. It had taken a couple of years to get out there again. If someone passed the lunch test, Grayson would invite her over for a late dinner or a movie at his place once his kid went to bed.

It wasn't much, he realized, but he was dipping his toe back in the dating waters and had been for the past three years. No one had sparked his interest enough to date anything more than casually.

The women he'd dated didn't stick around for long once they realized he didn't have anything to offer them other than a night here and there. Most thought him staying home to be there for his kid was adorable in the beginning, until they wanted to be taken out to a restaurant during dinner hours and he had to say that wasn't possible. Quite a few left in a huff, saying something about him being emotionally unavailable. He'd served the line *It isn't you, it's me* enough times to know it was truth.

"Okay, hotshot," she began, "What would you do if you didn't work for the FBI at all?" She didn't seem to mind putting him on the spot, but he'd asked for it. Her honesty was refreshing, though.

"I have never given it much thought," he admitted.

"Maybe it's time to consider a complete overhaul," she pointed out.

Grayson pulled into the parking lot of the motel and parked in front of their doors. Their rooms were next to each other. He cut the ignition off and turned to her. "Your grandfather…did he have any regrets for leaving it all behind?"

"Not one," she said as a small smile upturned the corners of her lips.

Grayson wanted to know what that smile was about.

# Chapter Eight

Grayson came around to the passenger door and opened it for Abi. She thanked him and then waited as he grabbed his own overnight bag from the trunk of his service-issued sedan. "I probably could have picked up my car when we drove past the crime scene a few minutes ago."

"It'll still be there in the morning," Grayson pointed out. "Or if we get back out to interview witnesses for ourselves."

"I was thinking we could go back to the party house once it's dark," she said. "Take a look at the possible angles where Max could have put down his drink. See if we can uncover how it all might have gone down. It's helpful for me to walk through it. But I can't stay up until one or two o'clock in the morning to do it."

"We can do that and we don't have to wait up that late," he said. "I usually do the same thing before too much of the dust settles around a scene."

"Really?" she asked, figuring if a legend like Grayson had similar habits, then she was on the right track in her career.

The sun was beginning its descent. It felt like lunch had been eons ago but it had only been a couple of hours. Time ticked as the day began to disappear into night.

"Yes," he confirmed as he closed his trunk and followed her to her room.

Once inside, he set up his laptop at the small table with a pair of chairs. Now that Abi could see clearly, the room reminded her of her grandparents' home. Floral curtains in purple and pink hues matched the bedspreads. Beige carpet led to a tiled bathroom. The place even smelled of rose petals. It had that warm, cozy feeling that made her half expect someone's grandmother to show up holding a plate of warm cookies. "What do you think about ordering pizza while we go over the files?"

"Sounds like a winner to me," he said.

"Do you mind?" she asked. "I need to shower and change into something more comfortable."

"No problem," he said but there was a husky quality to his voice that hadn't been there a few seconds ago.

Abi grabbed her overnight bag and headed into the bathroom, suddenly aware she was going to be naked in the next room. She was relieved her back was turned so Grayson couldn't see her cheeks flame three shades past red.

The bathroom was just as cozy as the other room, with its scented bath soaps and thick towels. There was a small basket filled with everything she might need, including a toothbrush wrapped in plastic with a tiny tube of toothpaste. This place couldn't be more adorable. Focusing on the details instead of her attraction to her coworker helped douse the flame. It had been too long since she'd been on an interesting date or in a relationship that lasted more than a couple of months.

Grayson was a father, which was the equivalent of a bucket of water on the burning embers. Abi repelled young kids. Her sister, Crystal, could handle them much better.

Not Abi. Her sister would tease her if she knew about Abi's attraction to a single dad. Crystal would laugh under normal circumstances. Abi doubted her sister would find much funny while keeping bedside vigil with their grandparents.

She slipped out of her shoulder holster and then removed her button-down shirt. The slacks came off next after she set her glasses down on the counter. She would need those for the next twenty-four hours at least while she gave her retinas time to heal. The last thing she wanted to do was pop in new contacts. After removing her undergarments, she turned on the water and then slipped into its warmth.

Fifteen minutes later, she turned the knob and wrapped herself in a towel. She'd packed sweatpants and a sweatshirt, so she grabbed those along with a sports bra and a fresh pair of cotton underwear before dressing. She spent the next ten minutes drying her hair before digging around for a hair clip that would keep it off her face and neck.

After twisting her hair and clipping it, she put on her glasses and then gathered up her dirty clothes. She placed those in the small laundry bag she had tucked in the zippered pocket. Once those were put away, she headed into the next room.

The smell of pizza wafted, causing her stomach to growl.

"I was just about to give you a shout to let you know food arrived," Grayson said as he set up paper plates and set a pair of Coke cans out. "Wasn't sure what you wanted to drink, so I got water and Coke."

"Caffeine sounds good if I'm going to stay awake long enough to check out the scene," she said on a yawn.

Grayson's shoulder holster was hooked onto the back of one of the chairs, his shirt unbuttoned. A man shouldn't look as sexy as he did with so little skin showing.

"I'm starved," Abi said, redirecting. She took a seat across from him and filled her plate with a couple of slices. "How did you know I liked every vegetable known to man on my pizza?"

"Took a guess," he stated. "We shared a meal already. It wasn't hard to figure out your preferences once you picked apart the menu." He brought his gaze up to hers for a split second and smiled. The temperature in the room heated up several degrees without either one touching the thermostat. "I hope Italian sausage is okay. I've never been a big fan of pepperoni."

"Well, that's it," she quipped in dramatic fashion. "I can't eat this. This is awful."

A mix of concern and disbelief flashed across his face.

"I'm just kidding," she added quickly. She hadn't meant to stress the poor man out. "I can literally eat anything on my pizza, but this is perfection."

Grayson shook his head and laughed. "I should have known. Who needs sriracha when you have that kind of spice around?"

They both laughed. Hard.

He was giving new meaning to words *dad joke*.

"That was bad," she finally said when she could stop laughing.

"The worst," he added. The man didn't mind making fun of himself. Add another amazing trait to the long and growing list.

If Abi dated coworkers, she would want it to be Grayson. Except for the kid part. She couldn't talk to anyone below the age of fifteen. Really. Plus, at twenty-eight years old, she would have been twenty-threeish when the kid was born. At that age, she'd been too focused on figuring herself out, which still applied. She'd finally gotten somewhat comfortable in her career.

"Did you ever think about the dangers of the job before you got married?" she asked Grayson.

"No," he admitted. "You?"

"I never even considered them," she responded. "Didn't then and don't now. But I also don't have anything to go home to like you do." Her life suddenly sounded empty, felt empty when she thought about it in those terms. This conversation triggered a deeper one that had been simmering underneath the surface for a while now. Abi's career was on track, but she couldn't keep a houseplant alive. The dead fern on the kitchen windowsill could attest to the fact. Her former boyfriends would also complain that she didn't "water" their relationship, to keep the metaphor running. She finished chewing the bite of pizza she'd taken while getting lost in thought, then asked, "Can I ask you something?"

"Shoot," he said.

"Don't take this the wrong way, but do you regret having a family?"

He picked his cell phone up from the table and then tapped the screen a couple of times before sharing. The picture of a dark-haired kid with short, spiky hair that had too much gel in it, and a small face and big glasses with red frames tugged at her heartstrings in a way no other kid had.

Looking at Collin made her ovaries ache, and more shockingly made her think she might be missing out on something big.

A WARM SMILE morphed the normally serious and sometimes sarcastic marshal's face. Abi was even more beautiful when she smiled. "Your son may be the cutest kid I've ever seen."

"Thank you. He's one of a kind." Her words and her smile warmed places in him that had been encased in ice far too long. If he went home and took a desk job, would that release some of the guilt that kept his dating life on ice too?

The annoying voice in the back of his mind said it was time to move on, get into a rhythm with his son's schedule. Be home for the kid. Teach him how to throw a ball if Collin ever decided to play sports. Or—and this scenario was more likely—Collin could teach his dad how to use all the tech gadgets. Grayson had always been an outdoor person. He knew the basics of using his phone and laptop. The agency had provided enough training for him to use those tools effectively for his job, which carried over into his private life. He had the basics covered.

And, hey, if his son wanted to play computer games instead of sports, Grayson wouldn't complain. All he cared about was having a healthy kid. Some outdoor time was necessary. Collin just hadn't found the right activity.

"Tell me more about him," Abi said but she was probably just being nice. She'd admitted to not being able to stand little kids. He now noticed a twinkle in her eyes that he hadn't seen before that was more like a longing, but he was most likely misreading her. When someone told you they didn't like something, experience had taught him that it was always best to believe them.

Setting aside the growing piece of him that wanted Abi to like his son, he decided to keep it short and sweet. "He likes pretty much all the Marvel characters. But the Hulk is his current favorite." Did his affection for the brainy scientist Bruce Banner, who turned into a big green hulk of a man when he got angry, have anything to do with Collin being picked on by some of his bigger, rowdier classmates?

"That's adorable," Abi said with a sigh. "I got picked on mercilessly for wearing glasses. Turns out kids can be ruthless with each other."

"He's had his fair share of insults hurled at him," Grayson admitted with a frustrated sigh.

"Makes me want to have a stern conversation with the parents of those bullies," Abi said with the kind of over-protectiveness usually reserved for parents. In Abi's case, she could relate on a personal level and tie it back to the harshness she'd suffered. Her reaction had nothing to do with Collin specifically. It was important to make that mental note because for a second, Grayson felt an intense connection to Abi that ran deeper than the sparks that flew between them when he stood too close.

"Makes me want to take those little twerps out back and give them a dressing down boot camp style," he couldn't help but say.

"You served in the military?" Abi asked.

"I did four years, which is how I got my degree," he said. The change in topic was good because he'd been known to overthink the bully situation with his kid, which in turn made him want to act on it.

"Thank you for your service," she said almost immediately.

"My pleasure."

"You want to know what I would do if I had a kid like yours and a job that required this much field work?"

He was surprised she was ready to offer an opinion, but he figured he knew what she was about to say, based on her earlier shock that he would consider changing his job. "Shoot."

Abi motioned toward his phone. "That face is worth staying home for. I get it now. Earlier, I was speaking from a place of not having a tie back home. No one needs me like he needs you. And, believe me, after being on the receiving end of being picked on, I know firsthand how much he needs you. I also know he's probably too embarrassed to tell you how much it hurts his feelings. And he might not even know the effects words like that have in the long run. You're doing the right thing in thinking about making a change." She flashed eyes at him. "Of course, what that change turns out to be is up to you. You need to be a desk jockey for a few years to be there for your kid. There's no shame in that. You can always get an adrenaline rush from jumping out of airplanes for fun."

He laughed.

"Funny to think that's actually safer than the jobs we do," he said. "If I was younger, I doubt I'd be having any of these thoughts of taking a step back. I'm forty years old. I've accomplished as much as I need to as a field agent."

"You're only ten years out from a pension," Abi pointed out. "I'm guessing you're beyond the twenty-year mark at that point." You had to work for the agency for twenty years and reach the age of fifty in order to receive a pension.

"Yes, I would be," he noted. "A decade is a long time."

"That's true," she said with a sneaky grin. "I'll be pushing forty by then."

"You'll be so old," he said after laughing.

"Ancient," she quipped, the spark returning to her eyes. "In all seriousness, Collin would be just shy of fifteen at that point," Grayson said. He'd done the math. He knew the policy.

"You'd only have three years with him before he went off to college," she surmised with a look of pity. "I see the struggle you have there." And then she added, "Having a family worth staying home for is a good problem to have, though." The statement caught him off guard as much as the look in her eyes when she said it.

"I may have been looking at this from the wrong perspective all along," he admitted.

Abi's cell buzzed. She finished the last bite of pizza on her plate as she checked the screen. "It's the sheriff. He wants to know if we can come to his office. He has a war room set up with volunteers looking through cell phone data."

Before he could respond, she said, "I'll tell him that we'll be there in twenty minutes."

# Chapter Nine

Abi changed into jeans, a blouse and a blazer before heading out to the sheriff's office. At least they'd had a break from thinking about the case for an hour while she showered and they ate. She was feeling refreshed and ready to dive back into the case.

The picture of Grayson's kid also reminded her why she did this job in the first place, to keep innocent people safe and lock up the bastards who would prey on others.

"We can pick up my car on the way back from the sheriff's office," she said to Grayson, who'd also shifted back into serious work mode.

"Easy enough," he said as she navigated them to the sheriff's office using the map feature on her phone.

The parking lot had a minimum of twenty-five vehicles parked in it. Grayson found a spot near the exit. The office itself was a small nondescript brown brick building, one-story. There was a larger building not twenty yards behind it, a jail.

A metal door opened to a lobby that looked like something out of the 1970s. Wood chairs and benches, beige patches of carpet, and a desk completed the room.

"You must be Marshal Remington and Agent Chisolm," an older lady who had stacked her gray hairs in a loose bun on top of her head said, standing up the minute they stepped into the room. "Sheriff Benton said to expect you." The older woman glanced at her watch. "You two are right on time."

Abi nodded and then shook the outstretched hand before Grayson did the same.

"I'm Inez," she said. "Pleasure to meet you." Inez had a sense of urgency about her kind and weathered blue eyes along with energy usually reserved for people half her age. "I'm Sheriff Benton's aunt. We run a small but tight ship around here."

Abi smiled at the beaming Inez.

"If you'll both follow me, I'll take you to the war room and let my neph...the sheriff know you arrived." Inez was a dear. She oozed small-town charm. Being related to the sheriff made sense as to why someone who looked like they should be a school librarian worked the sheriff's lobby instead.

The place had its charms and plants that were still alive.

Abi followed Inez down the hall to a conference room that had white boards on the walls and fold-up chairs around a conference table. There were tables lining the walls as well, with more fold-up chairs and folks studying screens, sometimes in pairs. She had to hand it to Inez: the place was quiet and organized. Maybe Inez missed her calling, considering she'd set the place up like a library.

"I'll alert Sheriff Benton of your arrival," Inez practically beamed before turning more serious. "Folks volunteered as soon as they heard about what happened." She had one of those time-worn faces that gave her an air of experience and intellect. "We're a good community here. When something happens to one of our own, we stick together." She lowered her voice. "Do you think he'll come back?"

"Only time will tell," Abi said honestly. "But we're going to do everything in our power to keep your citizens safe."

"We appreciate it," Inez said on a sigh. "It's just terrible what happened to that college boy."

Abi couldn't agree more. Inez excused herself and was off much like a tornado that touches down, spins around for a few seconds, and then bounces up and disappears. Of course, Inez didn't leave a destructive path in her wake.

Abi studied the walls. There wasn't much on them.

"Hey," a familiar voice came up from behind. "Looks like you two aren't afraid to roll your sleeves up and do some of the dirty work."

Abi turned around in time to catch Thad Carlson's sneer when he glanced at the back of Grayson's head. Seriously? Did the deputy not have better things to do than try to stir up more of his toxic masculinity?

"We're here to collaborate," Abi said before Grayson could respond. She expected him to turn and shoot a retort at the deputy. Instead, Grayson surprised her by leaning against the wall and folding his arms.

"Good to see you again, Deputy," Grayson said without a hint of sarcasm in his voice. The man was calm. The deputy was obviously feeling in his home turf here.

"Carlson, I told you to get out of here ten minutes ago to interview neighbors," Sheriff Benton said as he walked in, irritated.

"A lot of folks will be going to bed about now," the deputy countered. "Wouldn't it be better to swing by first thing in the morning?"

"You're almost guaranteed to catch them home right now," Sheriff Benton stated. "I don't care if they are wearing their pajamas or make you wait so they can dress. I asked you to canvass while information is still fresh in folks' minds."

"Yes, sir," came the deflated response. Deputy Carlson came across as someone who didn't want to be told what to do. He also seemed to have a problem with anyone who outranked him, unless of course you counted Abi. Did he see women as automatically beneath him?

Abi would be glad when they wrapped up the investigation here in town and moved on. The sheriff seemed fine, but Carlson was as a jerk and a creep. She'd come across her fair share of good old boys while working in rural towns. Thankfully, they weren't the norm any longer.

Carlson took off as the sheriff apologized for keeping them waiting.

"Was there something specific you wanted to show us?" Grayson asked.

"As a matter of fact," he said, glancing around and seeming to think better of having a conversation out in the open where his volunteer citizens could hear. "Would you mind following me?"

They did. The sheriff led them to the end of the hallway, to his office. It resembled the lobby but with leather couches, chairs and a better-quality oak desk that was massive. Behind the desk, the executive chair was flanked by a Texas flag on one side and an American flag on the other. Dead center was a picture of the governor. The office resembled many others she'd seen in her career.

The sheriff walked behind his desk and motioned for them to come with him. Abi and Grayson complied. She noticed her coworker was quietly taking everything in. He rarely spoke first. Even when provoked, he maintained a cool head.

Abi could learn a lot from the senior agent. It would be a shame for his agency to lose him, but after seeing the angelic, smiling face in the picture, she was certain Grayson needed to leave fieldwork. He would be an asset to any team with his experience. Sitting behind a desk might put him out of the action but he would still be contributing to putting perps behind bars. Wasn't that the ultimate goal anyway? Keep citizens safe from those who would prey on them?

The sheriff sat down and then entered a password before his screen came to life. "We got some pictures that might be of help. They're blurry when I blow them up, but we have someone working on filling in the pixels or whatever it is these computer wizards do."

That summed it up well enough for Abi's computer abilities.

"I thought it might give you a snapshot of the perp's movements, which is why I wanted to show these to you," Sheriff Benton said.

"We appreciate being brought in, Sheriff," Abi stated, which seemed to please the sheriff. He was tall, six feet one-inch at a minimum if she had to guess, and big-boned. The sheriff was probably in his early-to-midfifties, had a full head of white hair and plenty of sunspots on his leathery face and neck to indicate he didn't believe in breaking out the sunscreen. Inez was his aunt and was probably in her early seventies. If the sheriff inherited half of her energy, he would be just fine.

She also noted he was at the retirement age that would provide a retirement and pension for Grayson to be home with his kid.

The sheriff started bringing up pictures, one by one.

"See here," he said, going back and pointing to the

first. Blown up, the images were blurry, but a good computer guy should be able to fill some of that in. "There's a hooded figure moving along the fence on the east side of the property."

"I see him," Abi reassured. Too bad he never showed his face as the sheriff clicked through the pictures. There were photos of Max, looking inebriated as he talked to friends. Another showed him dancing. The red Solo cup was in his hand at one point as he held it up in the air while dancing on the edge of the yard near the fence. This corroborated Max's story about his activities last night. "Hold on." She saw something in one of the pictures with Max in the background holding his drink up. "Go back."

"Where? To this one?" the sheriff asked.

"Yes," Abi stated as Grayson leaned in. This close, she couldn't help but notice his unique, spicy scent. "Look at that." She pointed to the right of the screen. The picture was blurry. Whoever took it was most likely dancing themselves.

"I'll be darned," the sheriff said.

A hand hovered over Max's cup as he held it in the air. A gloved hand.

"The purple surgical glove," Grayson stated.

"You saw that too, didn't you?" she asked. "When the picture first clicked onto the screen, you tensed."

"I did," Grayson said. "It was blurry, so I wanted to see the others first, but this is a good find."

"We know the perp hung around in the background," she continued. "He wore clothing so dark that he blended in with the night."

"I'm guessing he either kept his gloved hands hidden in his pockets or put the gloves on last minute," Grayson said.

She wished they had something more to go on. "I haven't had a chance to write up my interview with the victim, but he remembered something after he spoke to you," she said to the sheriff.

"Oh," Sheriff Benton said.

"His mind is still foggy, and his memories can't exactly be depended on, but he believed that he saw a mole on the perp's neck," Abi said.

"The perp could have been circulating around the party at some point during the night," Grayson added. "Do you mind asking your volunteers to check for pictures of a male with a distinct mole on his neck?"

"Did he say where?" the sheriff asked.

Abi motioned to the spot. "The victim said it was noticeable." She also realized the kid was drunk.

"His blood-alcohol content was 0.18 percent," the sheriff informed them.

"Jesus," Abi muttered under her breath. That was seriously impaired to the point of the term *drunken stupor* to apply. This alone could cause Max to feel confused. Add a drug to it, and she was surprised he didn't pass out altogether right there on the lawn, making a spectacle of himself and dead weight for anyone who tried to carry him.

"I uploaded several reports to the shared folder about an hour ago," the sheriff continued.

Abi was still thinking about how the perp knew to act at just the right moment to get Max to walk away from the party.

"WE WERE JUST about to go over the documents when you texted," Grayson confirmed. "If you see any pictures of Max leaving, will you upload them to the shared folder?"

"Will do," said the sheriff.

"Thank you for contacting us right away," Grayson added. "It might be best if we took off so we can acquaint ourselves with everything in the files tonight."

"Yes, sir," the sheriff stated. Grayson appreciated the level of respect in the lawman's voice, especially after the conduct of his deputy. There had to be a story as to why Thad Carlson had a job. But that was a conversation for a later date and time, if at all.

The sheriff walked them out to the lobby and a smiling, waiting Inez.

"I appreciate you both for getting here so fast," he said after offering a handshake to Abi first and then Grayson. The man had a firm handshake and an honest disposition.

"Take care and if you need anything, give me a call," Inez said. "Even if it's just a recommendation for food."

"We will," Abi promised before heading out to the car with Grayson.

Once inside he started the engine and asked, "Did you notice what Max was wearing in the pictures?"

"A T-shirt and jeans," she said.

"A bright yellow T-shirt," he added as he navigated out of the parking lot. "That made him stand out."

"That's true," she stated. "We don't know what the other victims were wearing because they were found in just their underclothes."

"Which initially led us to believe they might have been sexually assaulted but that hasn't been the case so far," he added.

"I thought that was strange." Abi issued a pause. "In cases like these, sexual assault usually comes into play."

"Because the perp himself was victimized at some point in his life and acts out revenge on others," he continued.

"But this guy isn't assaulting them even though they are compliant."

Abi snapped her fingers. "The bowl cuts. He's acting out some type of fantasy that has nothing to do with sex." Max had escaped before the haircut.

"And everything to do with losing his power in some way." Grayson thought about the other victims. "I wonder if we can find a way to figure out if they wore some type of bright clothing that caught his attention."

"The team has been struggling to find a link between the victims other than the obvious ones of height, weight and hair color," she said. "This might be it."

Grayson might be digging here, but a small detail could lead to a trail that could find a killer. It sometimes came down to the little things in an investigation.

"It wasn't difficult for the perp to move around in the group," Abi observed. "And I checked time stamps on the pictures. There was no sign of him in anyone's pictures until long past midnight."

"Makes sense to go to a party that's already rocking," he pointed out. "Easier not to get noticed that way since, based on the pictures, this was a drinking crowd."

"There had to be someone sober at the party," she said.

"We can check the reports to see if anyone came forward as a designated driver last night," he mentioned as they reached the neighborhood. "At least we can retrace part of the perp's steps."

"What about the home's occupants?" she asked. "We should knock first. You never know when someone will sneak up on you with a shotgun in a small town like this."

"True," he said. "Keep your badge visible too."

"It's clipped on my belt, as usual," she stated. "But that's a good point. The faster we can identify ourselves as law enforcement, the better." She paused for a minute. "You don't think he'd come back to the site, do you?"

"The perp had to take off in a hurry," Grayson stated. "Which means he might have left something behind."

"The deputies on the scene would have collected any evidence," she reasoned. "We probably should have asked to see it."

"There will be pictures in the files," Grayson said. "We can get our bearings before we ask for anything individually."

"Good point," she said on a sigh. "But this guy is smart. He has already killed five times and my guess is that he's getting smarter each time, not the other way around. There's more attention on campuses now but I wonder how much that will stop him. Or if it will at all." She paused as a thought seemed to be bubbling up to the surface. "What if he hid something nearby?"

"Good logic right there," Grayson said, impressed. "He might have tucked a bag behind the garage or even in a neighbor's yard."

"Then he would have had to have scouted out the area a little bit to make certain there were no dogs that could alert folks to his presence," she continued along with the line of thinking.

Which meant he was most likely at his next location, starting the process all over again.

## Chapter Ten

Abi pulled her badge from her belt clip and palmed it as Grayson knocked on the door at 365 Armstrong Court. The small home had empty beer cans strewn in the fenced-in front yard. There was a trash can that overflowed to one side of the concrete porch. Grayson stepped back so Abi would be seen first. Everything Grayson did was deliberate, she'd noticed, so this move was meant to disarm the person on the other side of that door. Make them feel more at ease. Being tiny had its bonuses when it came to putting others at ease. Unfortunately, perps underestimated her, which meant they were more likely to fight.

A young man answered on the second round of knocks. His wide-eyed gaze immediately snapped to Abi's badge.

"We're sorry to bother you this late in the evening," Abi started. "I'm Marshal Remington and this is Agent Chisolm."

"Aiden Harker," the young man said, keeping the door cracked. He looked to be in his early twenties. His curly brown hair was a little too long. He stood maybe five feet nine inches and had a small build. He wore a wrinkled T-shirt and baggy sweatpants. His panicked expression said he was likely still reeling after what had happened in his backyard.

"We realize other law enforcement officials have been here, but we'd like to request permission to be on your property to assess the situation for ourselves," Abi stated.

"You can do whatever you want," Aiden responded without hesitation. "Just please find this person."

"That's what we're working on," Abi said. "We shouldn't take more than fifteen to twenty minutes."

"Do you want me to come outside?" he asked.

"No," Abi answered. "We're okay working by ourselves." She thanked the polite kid before stepping off the porch, turning on her cell's flashlight app, and walking through the front yard in search of anything out of the ordinary. "There's nothing here."

"No, there isn't," Grayson stated as he moved around with his own light.

"Local law enforcement would have walked all over the backyard, so footprints won't help us," she stated.

"It's still helpful for me to put myself into the mindset of the perp," Grayson explained.

She nodded, thinking the same thing. It was the way she liked to work. And she lacked confidence the reports would tell them much because she would have received a text or phone call if something important had turned up. Reading them later was solely about digging for nuggets of gold that might have been overlooked. Some things didn't mean much in isolation but put them together with other things and a picture emerged.

Being out in the field, examining the scene and every possible piece of evidence had always given her an edge. Interviewing Aiden was unnecessary because he'd been just as drunk as everyone else. He has been interviewed this morning not long after Max had been found and the young man remembered nothing. He'd granted access to his pictures immediately. His house was a regular party spot and he, as host, supplied alcohol to minors. Local law enforcement would have to figure out how they wanted to deal with him. Much of his cooperation most likely came out of guilt for Max and to save his own skin with law enforcement who could prosecute if they desired.

That, however, wasn't Abi's concern. Her only focus was finding the bastard who was looking to make someone his seventh target.

She and Grayson walked along the chain-link fence around to the backyard. Unsurprisingly, no dogs barked as the two of them made their way around the area. Abi crouched low to study the backyard. There was a wooden bar that looked like someone had made it from scratch. It was old and the wood wasn't in great condition after being exposed to the elements for years, but it was sturdy enough.

Based on her memory of the photos, she envisioned a yard bustling with young people who were dancing, spilling drinks all over themselves and others while others stood on the edges of the makeshift dance area and talked over the music. She retraced the steps of the killer, best as she could, based on the evidence they had so far. And then reenacted the chilling moment where a gloved hand come up and hovered over Max's drink—a drink that was raised in the air.

From here, the perp must have been watching for…how long? A minute? Two? The bright yellow shirt could have made Max a target. Aiden could have easily been the target with his dark hair and height. She wondered how much he'd been told about the situation and if he knew how easily this could have been him instead of Max? Black hair, or some variation thereof, made up more than 80 percent of Americans. Brown was the next most popular, coming in at roughly 11 percent. If those numbers held and there was a hundred people here in this yard last night, there would have been eleven candidates. Narrow that down based on height and the number would shrink.

Aiden would have been just as likely a target, so why Max?

The bright yellow shirt?

By his own admission, he kept to the perimeter of the party. Was Aiden in the center of it all? In the house? He'd banned everyone from coming inside due to carelessness with their drinks.

Was Aiden inside at the time the perp was out here picking his prey? An icy chill ran up her spine. This seemed like a good time to remind herself that going into the mind of a serial killer would always be creepy. It would always make her stomach turn and her skin cold. But there was a reason she put herself through it—to save lives. She switched gears to remind herself of the college students who were blowing off steam, making memories here. Their smiling faces, the group dancing was a way of connecting and dealing with the demands of tests and sometimes difficult classes or professors. Of course, in her mind's scenario they were all of legal drinking age. Not the case in reality, considering Max and many of the others who looked barely out of high school in the pictures.

*Why college students?*

"At some point, Max must have talked to the perp," Abi said to Grayson. "Right?"

"I was just thinking along the same lines," he admitted. "We should ask Aiden where he spent most of the party because he was just as good of a candidate as Max based on looks."

"Agreed," Abi said, moving back toward the front yard. She'd seen all she could out here. The homes on either side had the college-student decor of trash cans filled with empty beer cans and bottles along with kegs.

This whole street was most likely inhabited by college students, who were all part of the party scene. There was one way to find out, though. Go door-to-door.

Another thought struck. If the perp had ridden into town on a motorcycle, wouldn't someone have seen him? *Not necessarily.* Gas stations were pay at the pump. A helmet could have kept all of his head and most of his face hidden. He could have worn leather, which was common among the motorcycle set. It was chilly enough to get away with a leather jacket. So it was entirely possible he swooped into town unseen and without having to interact with anyone.

What about food?

If he stayed here very long, wouldn't he have to eat? Would he pack something and leave it on his motorcycle? He could have strapped something to the back. Also, some motorcycles had compartments.

A frustrated sigh slipped out.

Grayson reached out and placed a hand on her shoulder. His touch sent rockets of electricity firing throughout her body as warmth settled over her with the force of a tsunami. This man's touch impacted her entire nervous system, and her body wasn't exactly being subtle about its reaction.

"We'll find him," Grayson reassured her. The man had a sixth sense when it came to saying what Abi needed to hear in a particular moment.

She had no plans to give up before the bastard was behind bars. But would they find him before another life was lost?

GRAYSON KNOCKED AT Aiden's door one more time. The door opened almost immediately.

"We have a quick question for you," Grayson said to Aiden now that the young man seemed to have calmed down a notch.

"Okay," Aiden said. "I'm more than willing to cooperate. Ask me anything."

"This might seem like an odd question," Grayson started.

Aiden's lips compressed into a frown as he nodded.

"Can you show us the shirt you wore at the party last night?" Grayson asked.

"Yes," Aiden said, his face twisting in confusion. "I-uh-yes, I remember now." He disappeared before returning with a classic gray Old Navy T-shirt.

"Thank you," Grayson said. "That's a big help."

Abi stepped forward. "One more thing, would you mind walking us through where you were during the party?"

"The backyard," Aiden supplied.

"Can you be more specific?" Abi continued.

"Do you mean actually walk you through where I stood every moment because I had been drinking and I might not remember every step I took," he stated, crossing his arms over his chest to stave off the chill as he stood with the door open.

"If you could just give us the general area, that would be sufficient," Abi clarified.

"Do you want to come in and walk through the inside?" Aiden asked.

"That would be fine," Grayson answered.

The door opened wider, and Aiden backed away to allow space for them to walk inside. Abi walked inside first. Grayson followed into the living room. Wood floors creaked. Nails stuck up at odd angles from the old flooring that hadn't been attended to in far too many years. If these walls could talk, Grayson figured they would have plenty of stories to tell considering this place had the look—barely any furniture and he wouldn't dare sit down on the stained sofa—and the smell—stale pizza and beer—of a place that was rented solely to college students. The flooring was sloped. The living space small. A desk in one corner had a laptop on it and not much else. Notebooks like the ones he'd had to use were a thing of the past, replaced by technology. It made for less clutter, he had to give it that.

The kitchen had a fridge, an ancient stove with pots stacked on top of it, a sink with very little counter space. A small table with folding chairs sat to one side of the room.

Aiden led them straight to the yard and onto the concrete porch out back. He didn't bother to put on a jacket as he shivered, crossing his arms over his chest once again the minute he stepped outside.

"I mostly sat here." He pointed to the edge of the small concrete porch that was nearest the keg. "I was guarding the back door so no one slipped past me and destroyed the inside. I'd like to get my deposit back when I move at the end of this year."

"Did you find a new place?" Abi asked.

"Graduating," he offered. "If I can pass all my classes and don't get kicked out after this happened." A look of embarrassment crossed his features. "That makes me sound like a jerk. Max is a friend and I hate what happened to him, especially since it was here." He involuntarily shivered. "This whole thing creeps me out." His gaze darted around the fence line.

It was possible Aiden could have been in the perp's sights. He fit the general description the killer normally went for. He was the home's resident. Reynosa could have watched him come and go for days without Aiden realizing.

The perp was smart for changing up his location every kill. No one knew which campus he'd move on to next. There were more than 140 four-year colleges in Texas. Almost 500 options if you counted community colleges and trade schools. Given the location where the bodies had been buried, the assumption was that the perp only targeted campuses in west Texas. Only time would tell if the assumption was correct. So far, the northeastern Texas colleges had been safe. How long would the sanctuary last?

"Did you stay here the entire time?" Grayson asked. "Or circulate?"

"I didn't go far," Aiden admitted. "Couldn't trust people not to sneak in the house." He shook his head. "I knew I should stop throwing these parties. It's senior year and I'm too close to graduating to mess up my life."

There was a chance he was saying this because he was trying to get out of being arrested for allowing underage drinking to occur. But there was a sincerity to this young man's voice that was laced with regret. Grayson believed Aiden would probably blame himself for a very long time. It could have been so much worse.

"What happened here wasn't your fault," Grayson said reassuringly. "I'm not saying that you have no responsibility for the underage drinking. That is between you and local law enforcement."

"I deserve to go to jail," Aiden said. "My parents told me not to say anything until they sent a lawyer, but I didn't listen to them."

"What do your parents do for a living?" Grayson asked.

"They're lawyers," Aiden supplied. "I should know better." He waved a hand around the yard. "Right?"

"You're young, Aiden," Grayson pointed out. "This won't be the last mistake you make in life. But what happened to Max is not your fault."

"He could have died," Aiden argued. "I read the news…"

His voice trailed off like he couldn't find the words. Grayson wondered how much local law enforcement had condemned Aiden for the party. *Don't have the party and there wouldn't have been a crime* couldn't have been more off the mark but he could see someone like Thad Carlson making the statement.

"Still not your fault," Grayson said, a little more sternly this time. "You couldn't have known what was going on. Kids host parties around college campuses all the time. I'm not encouraging you to bring underage drinkers here." Grayson put his hand on Aiden's shoulder. "We've all done things we look back on and wonder what we were thinking. What happened here, though, is like lightning striking on a sunny day in New Hampshire. It's not typical and there is no way you could have predicted it."

Aiden's nod was slow, which meant at least some of Grayson's words were sinking in.

"I've been doing this job for a long time, Aiden. Believe me when I say there's nothing you could have done to stop someone in this town from becoming a target," he continued.

"He's right," Abi piped in. Grayson appreciated the show of support. "Don't blame yourself for what happened to Max. There are so many factors outside your control that led to what happened to him."

The argument was taking hold as Aiden's jaw relaxed some of its tension.

No one would know without interviewing the perp if Aiden might have been the original target. The bright yellow shirt Max had worn along with the fact Aiden never left the area right around the porch could have been factors in the perp's decision. As sly as this one was, Grayson doubted the perp would expose himself by leaving the perimeter.

"Did you meet anyone, by chance, who had a visible mole on their neck?" Abi asked as the conversation was winding down.

"No," Aiden confirmed after a quick headshake. "Not that I can remember anyway."

"If you should talk to anyone, especially a man with a mole, in the next few days, would you give me a call?" Abi asked.

"Yes, of course," Aiden stated. "Let me grab my cell so I can get your information."

He disappeared into the kitchen, returning a few moments later as Grayson looked out into the darkness. There were lights strung in a V, coming from the structure over the small back porch extending to the back fence where poles kept the lights high enough in the air not to interfere with the makeshift sixteen-by-sixteen dance floor.

As Aiden and Abi exchanged information, Grayson asked the young man to flip on the lights. He still hadn't figured out how the perp managed to talk Max into leaving. So far, there were no pictures of anyone being carried out.

The lights came on, brightening the backyard significantly.

"How well do you know Max?" Grayson asked Aiden.

"As well as anyone can know a freshie," Aiden said, then corrected, "freshman."

"Was he a frequent partygoer?" Abi asked, catching on.

"I'd say he was a regular," Aiden stated.

"How about drug use?" Grayson continued.

"I don't know," Aiden said as though trying to recall. "Drugs are banned at my parties because I'm not into that." Grayson believed the young man. When someone lied, there was usually a tell. Aiden would have to be an experienced liar not to give himself away or at least cause some doubt in Grayson's mind. "I can't recall ever hearing anything about him asking for drugs and I definitely don't remember him showing up looking high."

Drugs would have been an easy explanation for how someone could pull Max into the shadows. Plus, Max had been evading the truth when Abi had asked him about drug use.

Could a drug deal be the way the perp lured his targets out of the party once he dropped a drug—unbeknownst to them—into their drinks?

# Chapter Eleven

Frustration niggled at the back of Abi's mind. What was she missing?

After reassuring Aiden that what had happened to Max wasn't his fault, she thanked him for the information and asked him to get in touch with her if he saw a male with a neck mole around town.

Local law enforcement hadn't located anyone on a motorcycle in the area, and the perp was most likely long gone by now. Tension mounted with each passing hour because the bastard was already working on his next target. Abi knew it to be true and could feel it in her bones.

As they walked to Grayson's vehicle, she bit back a yawn and said, "It's late and we still need to stop by the garage."

"What about going back to grab a few hours of sleep?" Grayson asked, studying her as he walked her over to her vehicle. "I'll follow you back to the motel."

Abi bit down on her bottom lip, then scraped her teeth across it. Sleep sounded good right now. Her ability to think would be impaired if she kept pushing to stay awake. The killer would need time to regroup anyway. "Go ahead back to the motel." From the corner of her eye, she saw movement across the street from behind the houses leading in the direction of the garage.

With his back to the garage, Grayson must have read her based on her expression, because he turned so fast it made her head spin. Issuing a curse, he took off running. Abi easily passed him before they managed to cross the street.

Pushing her legs, she bolted toward the spot where she'd last seen the figure in between two houses. Pumping her arms, she ran as fast as she could, a burst of adrenaline aiding in her stride.

The dark figure easily hopped fences. He was four houses down, then five before she knew it and he kept going. From this distance, it was impossible to get a sense of height and weight, especially with the baggy clothes he wore. He was a runner, though. No mistaking that.

Their assumptions that the killer had left the area were blown out of the water if this was him. It made sense that he'd be back if he'd left something near the garage. Or was one of those animals who liked to hang around his crime scene. Some even joined a search for the missing person they'd killed. It was one of the reasons pictures or videos were requested by law enforcement at large gatherings or parks where youth sports were played, when a crime occurred. A perp could come across like someone who wanted to help.

It made Abi's stomach turn.

The runner hopped a back fence, heading in between a pair of houses. At this rate, he would disappear before she could reach him. Instead of following, she made a left and hopped the back fence. If she could see which direction he went, she had a hope of catching up to him.

Grayson's heavy breathing meant he was coming up from behind. Good. She wouldn't run off half-cocked without her backup this time. *Fool me once, shame on you. Fool me twice, shame on me.*

With Grayson close enough behind her, Abi rounded the house and turned to her right. Cars lined the street, but the perp was nowhere to be seen.

Had she lost him?

Half a dozen curse words fought for center stage as she ran into the middle of the street, scanning both sides. She pulled her weapon from her holster as Grayson reached her. With one look at her and a quick glance, he was caught up to the situation.

Grayson motioned toward the right-hand side of the street and then waited. He wanted to take that side. Abi gave him a thumbs-up, then she moved to the left. As near to the vehicles as they could be, they started walking. The road was eerily quiet. Abi didn't like this one bit. This kind of situation was dangerous. The perp could be any-where, including inside a vehicle.

He wouldn't be this close, though. No, he wouldn't circle back toward them. Would he?

Other than a streetlamp clear at the end of the street, it was dark. No porch lights were on. A few of the houses had windows boarded up. There was enough of a chill in the wind to remind her this was late October, and she could do with a coat. Without one, however, it was eas-ier to run.

Step by step, she and Grayson made their way toward the streetlamp. The perp had cut through the houses about halfway, whereas she and Grayson were only roughly one third of the way up the street.

The ease with which this person lost them made her think he might be local. Or someone who grew up here.

Spent time here at some point in his life. Could he have gone to college here?

Another car down, tension pulled Abi's muscles taut as she took another step closer. The perp could have gone inside one of the homes. He might be looking out a crack right now.

*Steady.*

Considering the possibilities had kept her alive this long. She and Grayson would have to call for backup before going inside one of the boarded-up homes. Taking time to make the call right now would give away her location and allow the assailant to move farther away if he was still on the street.

She and Grayson could work this together. Once they reached the streetlamp, she would call it in if there was no progress. The thought of this perp getting away tightened the tension.

As Abi took a step, a figure jumped out in front of her roughly ten cars ahead and pointed a weapon.

"US marshal, halt," she shouted with authority.

The perp fired a shot.

Abi didn't have her Kevlar on. A second later, she felt cold liquid on her left shoulder. She'd been hit? Her brain denied reality.

Ducking behind a vehicle for cover, Grayson identified them as law enforcement before firing a shot.

"Stop! Help!" The frightened voice belonged to a teenager. There was no way this could be the person they were looking for.

"Put your hands up where I can see them," Grayson instructed. His training dictated he defuse the situation. He wouldn't run to his wounded partner.

Abi checked her shoulder. Shouldn't she feel different?

Wasn't she losing blood? Instinct had her touching the spot where she'd felt impact. There was liquid all right. But unless she'd started bleeding green blood, the person who shot her hadn't used a real gun.

"It's a paint gun," Abi shouted. "I'm fine."

She peered around the vehicle in time to see the kid step out from in between two cars, hands high in the air.

Grayson had to treat the situation as if the gun was real. "Slowly, and I mean slowly, lower the weapon until it's on the ground."

The kid did. "I'm sorry. I didn't know. I thought you were someone else." He bent down and set the weapon down.

"Kick it far away from you," Grayson stated, moving closer with his gun still drawn. This wasn't the time to take chances.

Abi never understood why paint gun makers made them look so real. It was impossible to tell them from an actual weapon. Not all teens were smart enough to realize a law enforcement officer wouldn't be able to tell the difference. In her own hometown, a thirteen-year-old boy had been shot by a deputy after aiming a realistic-looking paint gun at the law enforcement official. She'd been in high school when the tragedy happened.

Grayson had the kid bent over a vehicle and was patting him down to ensure he had no hidden weapons. Abi took that moment to call the sheriff and report the encounter.

Sheriff Benton promised to have a deputy on the scene in ten minutes or less.

Abi joined Grayson when they were certain any threat had been neutralized. "What do you think you're doing out here shooting at a US marshal?"

"I'm sorry," the boy who looked to be fifteen years old

said as tears streaked his cheeks. "I wasn't trying to hurt anybody. Just having a little fun."

On the hood of the vehicle, there was a knife and a small bag of weed along with a pipe and lighter. The kid had dug a deep hole and Abi wasn't buying the tears. He might be sorry he got caught but he wasn't truly sorry.

"What are you doing out here at this hour?" Grayson asked. It was getting late, exhaustion was settling in as adrenaline faded, and Abi felt bone-tired.

"Hanging out," the teen said. He was face down on the vehicle with his hands clasped behind his back.

"What's your name?" Grayson asked as Abi inspected her shoulder. Sure enough, it was green paint.

She retrieved the paint gun for evidence. The kid was in more trouble than he realized. Or maybe he knew based on the way he was pleading.

"Riley," he supplied.

"Do you have a last name, Riley?" Grayson continued.

"Kline," Riley stated with a shaky voice.

"Do you know how much trouble you're in?" Grayson bit out.

"No, sir," Kline said. He wore baggy sweatpants and sweatshirt. He had on a black ball cap that he wore backwards.

"Do you think any of this is funny?" Grayson asked.

"No, sir," came the response.

"A deputy is on his way right now," Abi stated. "Soon enough your parents will be called in."

The threat was meant to score a direct hit. Instead, Riley's mouth twisted.

"Good luck finding my mom," he said.

This wasn't going well.

"SOMEONE WILL HAVE to pick you up from lockup," Grayson stated, holding his frustration back. He had no idea what would possess a young person to pull a stunt like this one, especially since shootings like this made the news. Grayson might have ended this kid's life over a paint gun. Naturally, he thought about his own son. Would Collin miss his mother so much that he turned out like Riley? Grayson wouldn't be able to stand himself if that happened. Collin was a good boy with a big heart. Didn't that mean he would end up a good teenager? "You need to tell us what you're doing out here."

"I was curious," Riley said. "About the...thing."

"Attempted murder isn't a *thing* to be casually thrown around," Abi said sternly. She had an air of authority that demanded respect and an intelligent, calm demeanor that said she deserved it.

"No, ma'am."

"Then, what? Why would you come sneaking around here this late at night with no one else around?" she continued.

"I just... I guess... I wanted to see it for myself," he managed to get out. His voice shook. He was nervous. Innocent?

"You do realize you fit the description of the kind of person the killer likes to target," Grayson ground out. This kid could end up a victim, creeping around to get a look at a crime scene.

Riley drew in a sharp breath. "No way."

"Yes," Abi reinforced. "Brown hair. Around your height. Would you like me to tell you what he does to his victims before he kills them?" Abi was intentionally providing information to bring a dose of reality to the kid in the hopes he wouldn't pull another stunt like this one again. He needed a wake-up call, especially if he didn't respect his parents. Not that all parents deserved respect. Grayson hadn't met Riley's, so he couldn't make a determination there. Many perps had a bad start in life. It wasn't an excuse. Plenty of folks had a rough beginning and still didn't end up on the wrong side of the law. But every hardcore criminal he'd arrested had a story of abuse or neglect that dated way back to childhood.

The more Grayson thought about it, the more he realized this needed to be his last case. He should probably pull himself off now that he realized what he had to do. But he couldn't abandon Abi.

"Coming out here alone could get you hurt in other ways too," Abi continued. "Possibly shot. You should know there are plenty of people who sleep with a shotgun next to their beds. If any one of them saw a dark figure lurking around, they could shoot. Everyone's nerves are on edge since last night." Abi might be coming down hard, but he was sure she wanted to make an impression on the kid. Grayson would be doing the same if she wasn't, in the hopes they could save this teen from doing something that could get him seriously injured or worse.

"I'm sorry," the teen whined, sounding more like a child than a teenager. Was it an act?

Grayson once heard from a former CIA agent who specialized in deception detection that every time a teenager opened his or her mouth, they were lying. The audience had laughed. He imagined many had teenagers of their own or at the very least experiences with them. Looking ahead to Collin's teenage years, which he'd heard would come faster than he realized, he couldn't imagine the sweet, innocent child morphing into someone he didn't recognize.

A deputy arrived, lights and sirens off, as the teen started to beg to be released.

"I identified myself as law enforcement and you still fired a weapon," Abi said. "You won't get off easy for that."

All innocence drained from the teen's face, replaced with bitterness. "Bitch."

Grayson's hands clenched at his sides. Abi's jaw tightened.

The deputy exited the driver's seat and joined them, breaking some of the tension. Abi gave a statement followed by Grayson. The deputy handcuffed Riley as he spewed more venom. All signs of the innocent teen were gone.

"That kid should get an Academy award for acting so innocent when he initially got caught," Abi stated as she checked the paint on her shoulder. Thankfully, it wasn't anything more than a large green splotch. But it could have been so much worse. Would she have survived? Absolutely.

Still.

"Are you good?" he asked her.

"Yes," she said a little too quickly. "It's just paint."

An incident like this one could shake up an agent or, in her case, marshal. Grayson had seen more than one decide to work desk duty after taking a bullet or coming close to one. Becoming aware of one's vulnerability could do interesting things to the mind, and mindset was everything while staring down danger.

"We can ride back to the motel in my car, if you would rather not drive," he offered. "We'll be back first thing in the morning anyway."

"Okay," she said. "We'll be joined at the hip."

If Grayson was going to think about the future and

about the possibility of actually dating again, he would like to find someone intelligent, thoughtful, funny and beautiful. Someone like Abi.

Shoving the unproductive thought aside, he walked back to the sedan alongside Abi.

The drive back was quiet. Abi leaned her head back on the headrest and closed her eyes. It was past midnight on what had been a very long day.

"Let's go over the files," she said the minute he cut off the engine. "My room okay?"

He nodded.

"I just need a few minutes to grab a shower in—"

"You can do that in my room so we can keep the conversation going," she said. "It'll be more efficient time-wise."

"Then, I'll grab my bag and head over." If this day was going to keep going, he needed to wake up. Best way to do that was a cold shower.

"I'll keep my door unlocked."

Grayson made a beeline for his room, grabbed his bag and then paused at his door to look at his cell phone. There was a text from Martha with a sleepy pic of Collin that tugged at Grayson's heartstrings. After tonight, he wanted to hang on to all that innocence for as long as possible.

Knocking once on Abi's door, he got the go-ahead to come inside.

"Shower is all yours," she said. She'd washed her face, pulled her hair back, and changed into the sweatpants and shirt she'd had on before the sheriff's text. She was sitting on the bed closest to the door with her laptop in front of her.

"Give me ten minutes," he said before heading into the bathroom.

True to his word, ten minutes later, he emerged showered, with brushed teeth, and wearing sweats.

Abi's head was back, her eyes were closed, and her steady, even breathing said she was asleep.

Not wanting to wake her but also not wanting her to wake with a crick in her neck, he set his bag down and helped her underneath the covers. He put the laptop on the table where they'd eaten dinner and then took the second bed next to the bathroom, wanting to be here in case she woke up at three o'clock in the morning and wanted to get back to work.

Being here with Abi felt like the most natural thing in the world. He hadn't had this feeling since Michelle. Even then, it hadn't been this feeling of rightness.

Grayson couldn't risk falling for someone who didn't like kids. Collin had to be the priority.

This attraction had to stop here.

"Stay with me," Abi's sleepy voice shouldn't be sexy as hell. She patted the bed next to her.

Against better judgment, Grayson joined her.

# Chapter Twelve

Abi woke to the sun peeking through the floral curtains and a sense of peace like she'd never known. She blinked her eyes open. Grayson was there. She was nestled into the crook of his arm, her right leg hitched over his left. Two layers of thick cotton kept them from touching bare naked skin to bare naked skin. But the heat pulsing between them caused the air to come alive, crackling with electrical current.

Reality was a hard bite because they weren't a couple and couldn't stay this way forever no matter how much her body craved more of his touch. An ache filled Abi's chest as she slid out from underneath the covers. She had a fuzzy recollection of asking him to join her last night after one helluva day.

Clothes on, no inappropriate boundaries had been crossed.

After freshening up in the bathroom, she put on coffee and grabbed a power bar from her overnight bag to put something in her stomach. She cleaned off the table following last night's pizza dinner. There were no leftovers, but the box wasn't the most pleasant smell first thing in the morning. Luckily, it was soon replaced with coffee. Much better.

Abi removed the box, taking it to the outside trash to get rid of the odor.

The sun was bright and the air crisp. All in all, the weather was shaping up to make it a beautiful day. In dark cases like this one, it was important to take a moment here and there to breathe fresh air and take in the warmth on her face. It was surprising how those little things could boost the spirit. Keeping up morale was important. Keeping a clear mind helped her come up with creative solutions. Staying away from a dark rabbit hole kept her sane and allowed her to do her job in the best way.

Between this case and the situation with her grandparents, she needed to find as many little moments as possible to get her through each day.

Speaking of her grandparents, she texted her sister for an update. The response came back immediately: No change.

No change meant they weren't getting worse. No change meant they weren't coding again. No change meant there was still a possibility of them waking up. What it didn't mean was they would have a meaningful recovery.

Abi thanked her sister for the update and then opened her laptop. She vaguely remembered falling asleep moments after she performed this same thing last night. The first update was on Riley from last night, who turned out to be fourteen years old, which was even younger than he looked. She could only hope he would wake up before he continued down a path that would lead him to jail down the road. Given his attitude, she feared the worst. Shame.

Next, she filtered through several reports that didn't tell her anything she didn't already know about the case. Then, she opened a document and started taking notes to filter through the important details, like the bright yellow shirt and the order of the campuses that had already been hit in search of a pattern.

A report from Julie said she'd called all campuses and had sent flyers. Most had agreed to pin them up in prominent spots on campus. It was something.

Julie had had no luck with finding out if any of the other victims had been wearing bright-colored clothing.

"Good morning," Grayson said as he sat up and stretched. His sleepy voice stirred a place deep inside her that didn't need to be stirred with a coworker.

Abi smiled and did her best to force down the attraction that had a mind of its own. "Morning."

"When did you get up?" Grayson asked. "I didn't hear you."

"You were out," she said. "I haven't been up long, though. I didn't want to disturb you."

"Give me five minutes and I'll get up to speed," he stated as he threw the covers off and then headed toward the bathroom. Being here with Grayson felt a lot like stepping into the sunshine after weeks of cloudy skies.

She got up and fixed him a cup of coffee while the sink ran in the bathroom. By the time he emerged, she had a cup ready to go. "Here you are."

Grayson looked taken back. "You didn't have to do that."

"I didn't mind," she said as he took the offering. "I can't believe I fell asleep." She shook her head. "There's an extra power bar in my bag if you're interested."

He thanked her for the coffee and then laughed. Reaching inside his bag, he pulled out a power bar. "Like minds."

Abi smiled. She didn't want to notice how in sync they were. Leaving Grayson once this case was over was already going to be difficult enough.

Grayson studied her after joining her at the table and polishing off his bar. He took a sip of coffee. "You look rested."

"I was running on empty last night," she said. "Thanks, by the way, for tucking me in and staying with me." She'd never needed that before from anyone, so she was certain it wouldn't happen again.

"Not a problem," he said but his husky voice told a slightly different story. Was he as affected by her as she was by him? There'd been a few signs here and there, but she almost convinced herself she was reading too much into them. Maybe even seeing what she wanted to see versus what was there. But the sound of his voice and the look in his said the attraction was mutual.

Not that it mattered. They lived in different cities. He had a kid. They had different lives. And after this case, they would have no reason to talk.

Or, could they be friends? Stay in touch at least on a surface level? She cared about whether or not Grayson decided to move on or stay in law enforcement. She cared about his kid and the bullying. As a matter of fact, once this case was over, she would like to meet Collin and tell him that he was going to be fine. She wanted to tell him the bullying wouldn't last forever and that it might even motivate him to find something he was good at and loved doing. She wanted to tell him that it was okay to stand up for himself.

Glancing up from her screen, she realized Grayson was still studying her.

"A whole conversation just played out across your face," he said. "Want to talk it out with me?" He must believe the conversation had to do with the case.

"I'm just forming thoughts," she said, definitely not wanting to share what had just happened in her brain. "It's just flashes, really. Nothing to discuss yet." She moved on by giving him a quick update on Julie. "She's doing everything she can from behind a desk."

"It's a huge help," he said. "We don't have time or re-sources enough to visit each campus in person. Sounds like she's covering a lot of ground."

"Part of me wishes we had time to educate these young people on the dangers of binge drinking after looking at some of those party photos," she stated.

"Did you party in college?" he asked.

"I went to a couple, but the scene wasn't for me," she admitted. "Plus, I was trying to graduate in three years since I'd taken a lot of college-level classes in high school. I didn't want to drag out getting my degree."

"Driven and beautiful," he said before catching himself. "No offense."

"Did you just apologize for saying I was beautiful?" she asked with a smirk.

"I did but I'm usually more professional than that," he stated, straightening broad shoulders.

"Can friends say something like that to each other?" she asked. "Because we decided to cross that line yesterday."

"Friends can absolutely remind a friend that she's beautiful," he said, returning the smile now. "It's only unprofessional for coworkers to cross a line like that with a compliment."

"Good," she said. "Because I need more friends, not coworkers."

He closed his laptop. "What do you want to talk about?"

"CAN WE SHIFT gears from the case for a few minutes?" Abi asked.

Grayson didn't mind. "We don't have any new information to go on and I don't fully wake up until my second cup of coffee. It's a good time to think about something else."

"Now that we're friends, I just wanted to say thank-you on a personal level," she stated. "You trusted me enough to talk to me about your son and your career."

"You're smart, Abi. I knew you'd offer a good perspective."

"And you trusted me despite the fact I have way less experience on the job and in life," she said.

"Doesn't mean you're not beyond your years," he countered. A slight flush to her cheeks made her even more attractive. "Don't doubt it for a second. Some law enforcement personnel that you'll end up working with the longer you stay in the business will treat you like you don't have a brain because of your looks. Don't let them get inside your head. Your instincts are sharper than anyone else I've worked with in my long and storied career. You might not have as many years on the job, but you understand what it takes better than most."

She gave a slight nod. Did she believe him? Or still have doubts?

Or was he on the wrong track?

"Can I tell you something about your son?" she asked, switching gears.

"Yes," he said. He'd already told her that he trusted her judgment.

"I've never been a parent and, honestly, can't say that I ever thought I would want to be one," she admitted before quickly adding, "I'm sure your son is amazing, though."

"He is."

"Keeping in mind that I have no experience with parenting, I still believe that Collin is going to be fine no matter what you decided about your job," she surmised.

"What makes you so certain?" he asked.

"He has you," she said. "And you're an amazing dad."

The statement shocked Grayson speechless. It took a couple of minutes for him to gather his thoughts enough to form words.

"When it comes to my job, I know I'm good at what I do," he started. "But parenting is a whole different ball game. Some days it feels like I'm swinging at every pitch trying to get it right. Others, the bat connects and I make it to a base or two. And then there are those days where I'm striking out at every pitch." He paused. "Does that make any sense?"

"I get the sports references," she said with a reassuring smile. "I guess I just wish you could see this from an outsider's perspective. Take, for instance, my parents. My mom also died during childbirth."

Those words were an arrow to the heart. "I'm sorry, Abi. I've been talking about my wife and how she died in the same manner without knowing how that might impact you. If I'd known—"

"There's a reason I didn't tell you before," she explained. "I don't remember anything about my own mother but hearing about Collin's, about how much she must have wanted him to be here, makes me think that maybe I'm not to blame for my mother's death. I didn't even realize I'd been carrying around that guilt until now." She took a sip of coffee before continuing. "But let me tell you, my father is nothing like you."

Grayson cocked his head to one side, wishing there was something he could say.

"He ditched us after Mom died and dumped us on our grandparents," she said.

"That's awful," Grayson said, his protective instincts jumping into action. "I honestly can't imagine any father doing that after he held his own child."

"Neither can any of us," she continued. "I'm the youngest of three children, in case I haven't mentioned that."

"I knew you had a brother, sister and cousins," he said. "I just wasn't sure how many of each."

"There's six of us in total," Abi revealed. "My sister is the oldest and I'm the baby. We have a brother, Duke, in between." She studied the rim of her cup. "Anyway, our father believed bringing up kids was too much work, so he took off and didn't visit. He didn't stay in touch by phone. We just suddenly didn't exist to him."

"The pain of losing a wife doesn't excuse shutting out those who need you most," he said as frustration any father could do that seethed.

"That's what I'm talking about, Grayson." She bit down on her bottom lip before continuing. "Your first instinct was to protect your son. You figured the best way to give him stability was to provide for him financially. Now that he's getting older and you feel like he might be missing you more or needing you more, you're contemplating quitting the job you love in order to be physically present for him. That's pretty damn amazing in my book."

Grayson had never thought about his situation in those terms. "Why is it so easy to focus on the areas where we feel like we're failing?"

"I don't know," she said, "but I can certainly relate."

"You deserve a better dad than the one you got," he said after a thoughtful pause.

"He has another family now," she said on a sharp sigh

before lifting her gaze to meet his. "And I have no desire to speak to the man again. I did hear that he called to sniff around about any possible inheritance after the accident."

Grayson flinched. "What a jerk."

"Truer words have never been spoken," she agreed. "But we had our grandparents, each other, and our cousins. I had the best childhood growing up on a paint horse ranch. As far as reasons to complain go, I got a bum dad. The other people in my life more than made up for it." She took another sip of coffee. "Collin has you. And you care about that little boy more than anything else in the world. He'll be more than okay in life."

Those words caused emotion to well in the center of his chest, forming a knot. "I hope you're right because he deserves the world."

"A kid that adorable deserves you."

Some of the weight on Grayson's shoulders eased. "If it's any consolation, I'm willing to wager your mother loved you more than you will ever know."

"From what I've heard from others in the family, she was an amazing person," Abi said, her eyes glistening with moisture.

"Then the apple didn't fall far from the tree," he pointed out.

"I hope I'm like her," she beamed.

"Based on what I've heard so far, you must have received your good qualities from her." He meant every word. "Your father is the one who is missing out, by the way. If your siblings are anything like you, he lost big-time."

Abi finished off her coffee after making eyes at him that said she agreed. Then came, "Do you think I could meet your son someday? It sounds like we have a lot in common and he seems like a great kid."

Grayson opened his mouth to speak but shock gave no words. His heart squeezed as an ache formed in his chest—a dangerous ache. One he couldn't afford to give in to while working on a case.

Abi had already been shot by a paintball. What if that had been the real thing?

Once a law enforcement officer saw the end of his or her career, sticking around put everyone in the vicinity in danger. Was Grayson a bad omen for this case?

## Chapter Thirteen

Abi had never once considered what she would do if she was shot in the line of duty. So, the line of thinking was throwing her off now. "You said you and Michelle never discussed the possibility of you being injured or worse on the job. Why do you think that is?"

"Superstition, for one," Grayson admitted. "Michelle said she got into a wreck after waking up one morning worried about driving when she'd just received her license. She had to block those thoughts out to get behind the wheel again despite the wreck not being her fault. It drove home a superstition, though."

"After one time?" she asked. "I mean, we all had those concerns when we first started driving."

"Her mom didn't help matters," he said. "She told me that she had a premonition about Michelle's death. She refused to see the baby for weeks, saying that he brought on a bad omen."

"She sounds like a piece of work," Abi stated.

"Her intentions weren't bad, but the woman was afraid of her own shadow," he said. "She always made predictions that didn't come to pass."

"Throw a hundred theories out randomly and one or two are bound to stick," Abi reasoned. "I guess I get it, but I've never been one to hide and superstition feels like hiding."

"How so?"

"It's a way of not facing what might happen," she said. "Not that I want to stay awake nights dreaming up scenarios about how I might meet my end on this job, but ignoring the possibility isn't realistic to me. Facing it, to me at least, is more of a *I see you, risk, and I'm taking you anyway because that will make me train harder and become better at what I do.*"

Grayson paused. A slow nod came as he processed. "I like it. It's logical. Avoiding a problem never made it go away in my experience. I just didn't talk to Michelle about it because it made her uncomfortable. But this makes a lot of sense to me."

"The paintball could be a real bullet next time," she said. "I have to face that fact and also acknowledge that I made a mistake not wearing my Kevlar."

"The paintball is the reason I've decided to change careers," he said.

"Ride a desk?"

"Or something like that," he said. "I have a little money saved up. I might have to be a desk jockey for a short time, but I don't see myself doing that for a decade. Hearing about your grandfather's business got me thinking about starting something of my own."

"What would you do?"

"I don't know," he admitted with a chuckle. Chuckles shouldn't be so sexy on anyone. "But it's time to face the fact that I don't want to travel anymore, and I don't want to go to a job I can't stand longer than I have to. I might have to do that for a little while until I figure out the rest, but I have other talents."

"Sounds like you're headed in the right direction," she said with more than a hint of pride in her voice. "Doing something you love is important considering we spend so much of our lives at work."

"Exactly," he agreed. "Being assigned to this case has been good for me in ways I never could have anticipated."

"And you found a new friend in the process," she said.

"The friend is the reason the case has been good for me," he said so quietly she almost didn't hear.

Rather than get inside her head about the implications of a statement like that one, she refocused on the laptop screen in front of her. They needed to shift focus anyway.

After a few quiet moments where Grayson set up his laptop and made a second round of coffee, Abi asked, "What are we missing?"

"I wish I knew," he said.

"There's no pattern to the murders," she said after studying the locations and their order. "One minute he's to the south, the other, he's to the west. And then he stayed sort of in that area before striking again."

"I'm not picking up on anything either," Grayson admitted. "There are no new pictures with the perp in the background from the volunteers. No new statements. We've already gone over the ones we have."

"Sitting around waiting for him to strike again is the worst feeling," Abi said, issuing a frustrated sigh. "We should get dressed and head over to the garage. See what we can find there that might have been missed."

"I just closed the folder with the pictures from the deputy on the scene," Grayson stated. "It's a small space but the report wasn't as thorough as I would have liked."

"Let's do this," she said, closing her laptop. And this time, she wouldn't be caught unaware. She intended to wear her vest.

THE WINDOWS OF the oversize single-car garage had been boarded up. Jagged glass stuck up from the sill. Abi followed Grayson past the yellow crime scene tape, wondering if the teen from last night had gone inside too. A move like that could implicate him in a crime. Maybe not this one since he couldn't have gone to all the campuses or carried the bodies. Would he know about ketamine? The internet made it easy for kids to learn way too much, way too early. Not all information was good to have for young minds.

The cold cement floor was stained with motor oil. Was there any on Max's clothing? Where was Max's clothing anyway? They knew his shirt was bright yellow because of the pictures, not because the clothing had been found.

An old convertible that looked to have been pieced out for parts sat on one side of the garage. This must be where Max remembered being in the back seat. "Why didn't the deputy take pictures of this?"

"Your guess is as good as mine," Grayson said, shaking his head. Shoddy work allowed far too many criminals to run free. Every law enforcement officer came to their job with different talents. Being good at details, however, should be a job requirement.

"He mainly covered the outside," she continued. "I didn't see this vehicle in his inventory list in the report either."

"That tells us everything we need to know about his level of detail and training," Grayson said with more than a hint of condemnation in his tone.

Small-town law enforcement had a reputation for being lazy but that wasn't fair to most in Abi's experience. Did some need more training? She would definitely say yes to that. Were they downright lazy? Not usually. There was the occasional Thad Carlson who seemed to skate by for reasons she had yet to figure out but most, as far as she knew, were eager to do a good job and liked having the chance to work with larger agencies. Thad was a piece of work. He wasn't the last chauvinist she would come across. Abi knew how to handle herself with jerks like him. The problem was they got in the way of a good investigation sometimes.

That was unacceptable.

"Thad's signature is on the inventory report," she said after checking the file on her phone.

"Figures," Grayson stated with more of that disdain. "He probably headed here after you turned him down for a ride to the motel."

"A guy like him likes to insert himself where he does more harm than good," she said. "Wonder why the sheriff puts up with him."

"Could be a relative who needed a job," Grayson reasoned. "Sheriffs are elected, and we already know Benton hired his aunt to work in the office."

"True." She walked through the mostly empty space, checking for other items not listed on the report. In actuality, very little was listed. Did Thad miss these items out of laziness or negligence?

Grayson dropped down on all fours, checking underneath the vehicle that was up on blocks. "Do you think the perp would've stayed here after Max escaped or gone after him?"

"Gone after him," she suggested. "I wish we knew how Max got away from him."

"Could have swung at the guy, connected, knocked him off of him and ran this way." Grayson reenacted the scene without getting inside the car.

Abi moved to where the perp would have fallen. Sure enough, a bucket that was tipped on its side looked like it had been knocked across the floor by someone. She got out her camera and started taking her own images. "Go through those motions again for the camera."

Grayson did as she stared at the screen to ensure she got a good video. A figure moved past one of the larger cracks.

"Grayson, someone is out there," she said to him before motioning.

He immediately pivoted toward the door and raced outside.

The squawk of a radio met her as she stepped into the cool air. Abi stopped cold. "Deputy Carlson, we were just talking about your report."

GRAYSON TOOK A step back, ready to watch a pro at work. Abi was a force to be reckoned with and he had a feeling Thad Carlson was about to be on her bad side.

The deputy's defenses came up as he practically sneered at Abi. *Wrong move, buddy.*

"What about it?" Deputy Carlson asked in practically a growl.

"I'm curious as to why a lot of inventory was left off the list," she stated. Abi spread her feet in an athletic stance as she seemed to stand taller than her roughly five feet two inches. Grayson smirked. He couldn't help it.

"I didn't see the relevance of some of the items," Deputy Carlson defended. "When I do inventory, I only mark what is important to the case." He spread his feet, mimicking her movements. Was he trying to establish dominance? *You are so lost right now, dude.*

Abi issued a grunt, but otherwise came across as unbothered. "What makes you think you know what is and isn't relevant to a case this early in the game?"

"Maybe your brain is still fuzzy from taking a face full of pepper spray," Deputy Carlson started. "So, I'll go easy on you, little lady. But you need to learn your place before—"

"Care to enlighten me?" Abi asked, maintaining her cool despite Deputy Carlson trying to bait her into an argument. "Exactly what will you do, Deputy? Because last time I checked, keeping an item off an inventory list that could be sold or used personally meant interfering with a federal officer's investigation." She took a step closer but didn't raise her voice. "Have you met my partner, Federal Bureau of Investigations Agent Grayson Chisolm?"

Deputy Carlson's cheeks turned a shade of red equivalent to a wildfire. The heat radiating from his glare matched the intensity of his expression. "Look here, little lady. I'm not about to—"

"What, Deputy? Have to explain yourself to an entity that you don't have an inside line on?" she quipped. "We already know about your special in with the sheriff. Do you really think the US Marshals Service cares the two of you are related? Or the federal government? Blood only gets you so far when you abuse your position."

Carlson's face turned pale. His jaw dropped. The man wasn't very good at hiding his reaction when he got called out.

Abi took another step toward him until they were two feet apart. Not close enough to be in his face but enough to let him know she meant business. Fists clenched at her sides, she was a ball of energy that could explode on the deputy at any second. Her voice, however, was a study in calm.

"Well, now, hold on there," Deputy Carlson's disposition flipped on a dime. Abi's dime. "Let's not get our panties in a bunch."

Abi leaned back like a cobra about to strike. "Word of advice, Deputy?"

Carlson nodded as sweat formed on his brow. His pulse must've kicked up, because he was breathing like he'd just sprinted across the street instead of walking slowly like he usually did. He started blinking rapidly, another telltale sign of guilt. Abi had hit on something that made the deputy uncomfortable. Nepotism? Squirreling away evidence on a crime scene instead of reporting it so it could be sold later? Used for personal gain? Or just used personally?

"Go on," Deputy Carlson said to Abi. His body language told a different story as he touched his belt for the third time in less than a minute.

"Look me in the face when you talk to me because my mouth isn't down here." She motioned to her chest area. "Drop the words *little lady* out of your vocabulary or you'll be brought up on sexual harassment charges. And, finally, never mention my undergarments when you address me. My name to you is Marshal Remington or ma'am. If you don't respect me or the badge, have a little respect for yourself. Speaking down to a female colleague or making derogatory statements isn't flattering and could be cause for you to be forced to turn in your own badge. Now, you need to ask yourself an important question. Do you really want to take on the US Marshals Service or the Federal Bureau of Investigations?

The deputy's jaw dropped. He wasn't used to speaking to a female colleague who could hold her own. He closed his mouth with an audible snap. "Are you intending to make a report, ma'am?"

"About the evidence missing from the initial report? Absolutely. As far as the rest goes, mind your p's and q's and I'll consider giving you the benefit of the doubt this time." She stood her ground. "Be on notice that if I hear one more demeaning statement, I fully intend to file every possible complaint against you and your department. Understood?"

Deputy Carlson stood at attention. "Yes, ma'am."

"Now, do you want to clue us in as to why you left the items off the report?" she asked.

He leaned back on his heels. "Didn't think they were relevant," he said as he touched his belt again.

The man had just lied.

# Chapter Fourteen

"What else didn't you 'think' was relevant?" Abi asked the man who'd tried to push every one of her buttons. His reaction to her line of questions, however, told her that he was lying. At this point, she needed to make certain he wasn't covering anyone else's tracks.

Did he have any links to the towns where the other murders occurred? Abi made a mental note to find out.

"Just what you saw there," Deputy Carlson stated. His demeanor changed and he treated her in a professional manner now. If nothing else, that was a win. Men like him were relics left over from a different time—and that time was up.

Was he involved in negligence or criminal activity?

One had a little more relevance to the case.

"Here's a suggestion," Abi started. "Why don't you go back through the garage and catalog every item? Then file an amended report to include the items you missed on the first go round?"

"Yes, ma'am. I'll do that right now." At least the deputy knew better than to argue at this point.

He waited for her to give the go-ahead before walking away and entering the garage.

Grayson moved next to her and said in barely a whisper, "Well done."

It meant a lot to hear him say those words. "Thank you."

"No one should have to put up with that kind of bias," he continued as they walked away from the garage. "I feel confident he'll watch his words moving forward. Future women will have you to thank."

"He was lying, though," she pointed out.

"I caught that too."

"Do you have a guess as to the reason?" she asked.

"Since you and I think along the same lines, I doubt I have anything more to contribute than you've already figured out," he conceded. "I went with covering someone's tracks, being too sloppy with his work, and wanting to use or sell the items off the list. Mainly the vehicle. Old cars like that can be sold for parts."

"And if there's no record of the vehicle, no one can trace it back to him," she said before issuing another grunt. "It's deputies like him that give small-town law enforcement a bad reputation."

"Couldn't agree more." Grayson pulled out his cell and typed in *Carlson* along with the name of the town. "I got a hit. Check this out." He tilted the screen so she could read it better.

*Carlson Auto Repair.*

"Hell's bells," Abi said. "Guess it didn't take a whole lot of detective work to figure out what the 'good' deputy intended to do with the convertible parts."

"It's big business to find out-of-stock parts for old vehicles," he pointed out.

"I'm guessing Carlson gets a cut on the back end," she said with a tsk. "He just gave us no choice but to report him."

"My thoughts exactly," Grayson said. "I'd offer to write up the report myself, but I think you'd enjoy it more."

"There's no room for criminals in law enforcement," she stated. Period.

"A small few sure make our jobs difficult as hell," he said on a frustrated sigh as they circled the perimeter of the garage outside of earshot.

"If we dig a little deeper, my guess is that we'll find out that the sheriff and the deputy are related." Abi didn't like nepotism. Too many times the relationship was taken advantage of by one of the parties. In this case, her money was on the deputy. She usually got a feel for people. The sheriff came across as honest. The fact wouldn't stop her from looking into his background to make certain.

As she surveyed the area, a bright yellow fabric dot caught her eye. "I might have spotted something." Before she finished speaking, she was already making her way toward the dot as Grayson walked by her side.

The dot led them to the back of an abandoned dog-house tucked in the back of the neighbor's yard next to a tall mesquite tree. This was the reason she always investigated a crime scene for herself. In the moment, it was too easy for a law enforcement officer to miss a critical piece of potential evidence. The shock of a crime like this happening could throw a decent deputy off. Having someone like Carlson around didn't help matters as he probably volunteered to take what he would consider the easiest job of walking the perimeter in search of clues.

The doghouse was in poor repair. Meant for a large dog, it stood five feet high and had a shingled roof. It also had a few flaps at the door like most dog doors in homes did. The flaps were black rather than clear, which would keep out the sun but also made it difficult to get a look inside without touching them.

Abi pulled a pair of gloves from her back pocket and

slipped them on while Grayson looked around on the ground for something to use to open the flaps.

He located a stick and then flipped on his flashlight app.

Abi crouched down and checked behind the doghouse. She took the bright yellow fabric piece—fabric was notorious for not holding prints so she wasn't worried about touching it—and then reached behind. "There's a large hole in the back of the doghouse. And the chain-link fence has a hole big enough to fit a box or bag through."

"Can you determine if the fence cuts are recent?" he asked, kneeling beside her.

"No," she admitted. Either the perp had cut the fence, or it was already there, and he'd taken advantage of it. "Coming from the back like this wouldn't leave obvious tracks in front. Most deputies would skim the area looking for the obvious." It was a smart move on the perp's part to come from behind, if that was the case.

"What about the fabric?" Grayson asked.

She held it out on her palm. "Not much more than a swatch." The piece covered her palm. It was ripped, not cut with scissors. Hastily?

"Souvenir?" he asked the second she thought it.

"I'll check the front," he said as she trailed a step behind.

Using his phone, Grayson turned the flashlight app on. The sun was high in the sky at this point but inside the doghouse would be dark based on the size of the opening and location of the sun overhead. Plus he wouldn't be able to see far without additional light. He crouched down and pulled the flaps back.

"Bingo," he said almost immediately.

"What did you find?" she asked. She'd been unwilling

to stick her hand in the dog shelter from the back, considering all the spiders and who knew what else that might be crawling around inside.

"Hold on," he said as she joined him up front. He had to lean in so far that his torso disappeared. He came out with a beaten up camo lunch-type bag, using a stick so that he didn't get any fingerprints on the straps.

"We need something else to pry it open with," Abi said, immediately searching the ground for another stick to use. Even gloved, she didn't want to risk the possibility of wiping away any fingerprints that might be on the strap or bag.

The usual adrenaline rush that came moments before a big case might break wide open slammed into her. Pulse racing, she located a stick and controlled her breathing to slow, measured breaths to stop her hands from shaking.

Grayson caught her gaze. "Brilliant work so far, Abi." The way her name rolled off his tongue sent goose bumps up and down her arms, radiating through her body. The compliment from a seasoned agent meant the world.

"Thank you," she said. "Now let's see if we can find something inside this bag to stop the bastard before he kills again."

A meticulous killer like Reprehensible wasn't likely to leave an obvious trail. Not even now. Could they find a trace that could point them in the right direction? The tip line had been flooded with calls, according to one of the reports Abi read this morning. Not uncommon in a high-profile case like this one. Sorting through them to find a nugget of gold wouldn't be easy.

Could they catch a break here?

"Ready?" she asked Grayson.

"Let's do this," came the quick response.

Each used their stick to pry open the opening of the bag using opposing force.

Abi used her gloved finger to expand the opening. The triangle approach gave them a view to the contents.

Five fabric swatches of varying bright colors were the first things she noticed. "Souvenirs," she said under her breath.

"That's something we didn't know before this case," Grayson stated. "The bright colored shirt theory was on point."

"True," she agreed. "Should we dump the rest onto the ground?"

"Carefully," he said with a nod after making eye contact. "Since this was your find, why don't you do the honors?"

Abi took hold of the bottom of the bag before shaking it out gently. A small horde of protein bars fell out, all stuffed inside Ziploc bags. An unopened water bottle tumbled out from the bottom of the bag.

Abi turned the bag over. They opened it again with the sticks. A piece of paper stuck to the bottom of the bag, caught in the seam. She didn't dare assign too much meaning to it. "Could be nothing."

She made eye contact with Grayson. The look on his face made words unnecessary.

"I know," she agreed because they both knew one little object like this could be the puzzle piece they'd been searching for. Using the sticks as chopsticks, Abi pulled the paper out with the kind of precision used when someone was scared they might topple a Jenga puzzle over, causing all the pieces of wood to come crashing down around them.

With the makeshift chopsticks, Abi was able to pull the piece of paper out. It was an article from the *Daily Texan*.

Abi set the crinkled-up page on the ground. Using the sticks, she and Grayson flattened the paper out so they could read it.

"It's about him," she said with an eerie feeling. "What do you think the odds are that he's going to strike at UT Austin based on this?"

"I'd say it's time to check out of our motel, notify our supervisors and get on the road to Austin."

"UT is known for being a party school," she pointed out. "Even if we get there in time, how on earth will we figure out where he'll strike?"

"We can brainstorm ideas on the road," Grayson said as they meticulously placed evidence back inside the bag.

"Who do we trust with this?" Abi asked.

"No one here," Grayson decided. "We'll call this in once we get on the road to Austin and see who we can get to either meet us or tell us where a good drop spot would be. I don't trust anyone in this department to handle evidence properly after what we saw in the garage."

"Agreed," Abi said as they pushed to standing. With the stick looped through the bag's strap, they made a beeline toward their vehicles. "I'll follow you back to the motel."

"Sounds good," Grayson said. "You take the evidence since this was your find."

Pride brought a smile to her face that faded too quickly. It was a shame Grayson was leaving fieldwork. She could learn a lot from someone like him, not to mention the fact they made a good team.

Friends would have to be enough.

Abi reached her vehicle, and then pulled out an evidence bag so as not to taint anything. After placing it inside with the kind of care usually reserved for handling expensive and breakable artwork, she set it down on the floorboard of the passenger side.

She tried to start her engine, but nothing happened. *What the...?*

Abi hopped out of her vehicle after hitting the button to pop the hood. She exited as Grayson caught on, joining her.

One look inside had him swearing.

"What is it?" Abi asked, scanning under the hood. And then she saw it too.

# Chapter Fifteen

"Your battery cables have been cut," Grayson said to Abi.

"What the actual hell?" she asked. The question was directed to no one in particular. "I'll send a text to the sheriff and see if he can lean on the teenager from last night. Riley might have pulled something like this."

"He was my first thought too, but to what end?" Grayson asked.

"Other than being a twit and not realizing the consequences of his actions?" she asked. Her frustration made her cheeks flush. Anger did that to her the same as embarrassment, he'd noticed.

His first thought might have been Riley but how would the kid know which car was hers? "Find out where he lives, would you?"

Abi already had the sheriff on the line. She asked for Riley's home address then rattled it off to Grayson. He pulled up the map feature on his phone and input the address from memory. The place was several blocks away. It would have been impossible for him to watch the investigation unfold from inside a window as Grayson suspected might have happened.

Deputy Carlson stepped out of the garage. He glanced over, stopped. Then, must have decided it was worth the walk over to find out what was going on. "Everything all right over here?"

"Marshal Remington is having car trouble," Grayson supplied, wondering if her car would be towed to his relative's repair shop.

"I know a guy who can help," the deputy said.

"Any chance this person is a relative of yours?" Grayson asked.

"My cousin owns a place," Deputy Carlson stated. "He can tow the vehicle and fix the li... Marshal Remington right up. No charge."

"The Marshals Service would cover any cost associated with the repair," Grayson pointed out. "Your offer to help is much appreciated, though." Was the man trying to redeem himself because he'd been called out over his shoddy work? Was he trying to butter them up? On a hunch—a hunch honed by years of field experience— Grayson asked, "You didn't happen to see any suspicious person or persons around Marshal Remington's vehicle while working out here, did you? I know it's a long shot but just in case."

Deputy Carlson touched his belt. "No, sir. I did not." Damn liar.

Was the deputy trying to force Abi to use him for a ride? Was he that desperate to get her inside his car for some alone time? Did he think this was appropriate?

Grayson already had the answer to that question. When it came to the opposite sex, the deputy had no idea how to treat them as equals. He didn't view women as colleagues. And, based on his actions so far, thought all he had to do was get Abi alone for five minutes to charm her.

Carlson walked a narcissistic line bordering on criminal. Then again, his actions so far said he wasn't afraid to bend the rules for his own gain.

Going by the narcissistic line of thinking, Deputy Carlson could have cut the battery cables himself to punish Abi for not taking him up on his offer. This was the type of guy they were looking for if pushed to an extreme. Reprehensible didn't differentiate between sexes, though. He was looking for a type. He was looking for bright clothing.

This thing with Deputy Carlson needed to be shelved for the moment so as to be not distracted from the case. Studying the man right now, Grayson had his answer. Carlson had either cut the lines or had had them cut to get back at Abi. Plain and simple.

Grayson would call the sheriff on the road to get a feel as to whether he knew what kind of deputy he'd employed. If the sheriff was in on it, which Grayson doubted, he'd ensure the department underwent an extensive federal investigation. For the moment, however, he would feel out the sheriff.

Walking away without reporting Deputy Carlson's actions wasn't an option.

Shifting gears for the moment, Grayson thought about the motorcycle. Since he'd been in town, he'd counted half a dozen. Most were easy rider types. He hadn't seen any crotch rocket types.

If he had time, he would stick around and interview anyone who lived near the highway. He would check in with businesses too, just to see if anyone saw a male on a motorcycle. Pulling records to find out how many Class C licenses belonged to males in Texas would be like looking for a needle in a haystack. It would waste precious time—time that was running out with each tick or tock of the clock.

"Don't worry about Abi's vehicle," he finally said to Carlson. "I'm sure the Marshals Service will send a tow." He made a mental note to remind Abi to tell her supervisor not to allow her vehicle to be picked up by Carlson Auto Repair.

"Let me know if there's anything I can do to help," Deputy Carlson said.

"An amended inventory list is a good place to start," Grayson stated.

"I'll get that filed first thing," the deputy promised.

Abi had made two calls in the duration of Grayson's conversation with the deputy. The first had been to the sheriff. The second had been to her supervisor.

"How much of my conversation did you overhear?" Grayson asked.

"Pretty much all of it," Abi admitted. "The lying bastard."

"My thoughts exactly," Grayson agreed. "We'll deal with him later. In the meantime, what does your supervisor want you to do?"

"I asked if I could catch a ride with you to Austin," she informed. "Hope you don't mind."

"I'd prefer it," he said. "Makes it easier for us to talk on the road."

"I'll just grab my things out of here and then we can swing by the motel." She closed the hood and then started toward the driver's side. "By the way, I believe the sheriff has no idea what he's dealing with." She tilted her head toward Deputy Carlson, who'd slipped into the garage.

"I get the same impression," Grayson said.

"My supervisor is having a tow pick up my vehicle to have it repaired in a bigger city," she added.

"Good."

Grayson helped remove the last of the items from Abi's vehicle before she emptied the trunk. There was an arsenal of weapons back there including a shotgun and enough ammunition to last a week in a shootout.

"Ready to roll?" he asked once her vehicle was emptied and locked.

"Let's do this," she said, echoing one of his most used lines. The knot in his chest tightened at the thought of not working a case with Abi.

Or being able to talk to her on a whim.

Grayson realized he was in trouble when it came to the dark-haired, feisty beauty. He just didn't know how much until now.

FORTY-FIVE MINUTES AFTER climbing into Grayson's passenger seat to drive back to the motel, Abi claimed it once again for the next leg of their trip. The drive to Austin on US 87 S and State Highway 71 would take a little less than five and a half hours.

"How hungry are you?" Grayson asked once they'd been on the road twenty minutes.

"I could eat my shoe, but my stomach will kick back another power bar," Abi admitted with a laugh.

"Do you want to check for the nearest fast-food chain?" he asked.

Abi pulled out her cell, then muttered a curse. "How did I miss this?" A missed call from Crystal sent Abi's stomach churning. She immediately called back, noticing the call had come in more than fifteen minutes ago.

Crystal picked up on the first ring. "Hey."

"Good news or bad?" Abi immediately asked.

"Grandma Lacy opened her eyes and squeezed my hand," Crystal reported. "I immediately hit the nurse's button but by the time the doctor showed five minutes later, Gran was unresponsive again."

"What does that mean?" Abi asked.

"That this is going to be a roller coaster," Crystal stated on a heavy sigh. "The doctor explained that ups and downs like this one are not surprising. Recovery is generally not a linear proposition."

"Was this a good sign at least?" Abi asked, trying to find a positive thread to hang to on to.

"It's not a bad one," Crystal said. Clearly, her sister didn't want to set up false hope. Then came, "I'm sorry that I don't have better news. We're all hoping to get some kind of sign at this point."

"Sounds like we have reason not to give up hope," Abi said, trying to lift her sister's spirits. "Wish I was there."

"There's literally nothing you can do," Crystal pointed out.

"I could keep you company," Abi countered.

"Wade's been a rock," Crystal said. How had Abi so easily forgotten her sister was no longer alone? She'd been so stuck in her own head, in the investigation that she'd almost forgotten about her sister's fiancé.

A stab of jealousy mixed with happiness that Crystal had found the one.

"Wade sounds like a great person," Abi managed to say with forced enthusiasm. She couldn't be happier for Crystal and Wade, but she would like to meet her future brother-in-law face-to-face at some point.

*When this case is over.*

"I think you're going to love him," Crystal said.

"Probably not as much as you," Abi said, forcing a smile she didn't feel. She wanted to be happy for her sister and she was, but most of her couldn't get past the stress of not being at the hospital. Guilt stabbed at the thought she could so easily block out everything but the case until she was reminded of it by her sibling.

"He's special to me," Crystal said. From the sounds of it, she was just as guilty of pretending not to be down about their grandparents.

"I'm glad the two of you found each other," Abi added. "You deserve a great partner, Crys."

"So do you," Crystal said, then quickly added, "Don't feel guilty about not being here right now. Okay. I was in the same shoes as you not long ago and I know how difficult a position you're in. Give yourself a break. Okay, Abs?"

Only her sister ever got away with calling her that. Vice versa, she was the only one who called her sister Crys.

Moisture gathered in her eyes at the thought of ending the call with her sister. Abi was not usually the emotional type, so they caught her off guard.

"Thank you for being at the hospital, by the way," Abi said, hoping her sister knew how much having Crystal there made it easier for Abi to focus on doing her job.

"I hope you catch the bastard you're after soon," Crystal said. "And not just because I want you home. Though I do."

Abi understood completely what her sister was saying. They were both US marshals. Hell, the whole family worked for the Marshals Service. They all most likely had their grandfather to thank for that.

"He called again," Crystal said. The note of anger in her voice clued Abi in.

"Dad?"

"Yes," Crystal confirmed.

"What did he want?" Abi asked with a sour taste in her mouth.

"He's acting like he's concerned but I think Duke was right about the man fishing around to see if there's going to be an inheritance," Crystal said.

"That's up to our grandparents but the man doesn't deserve the time of day if you ask me," Abi said.

"He called Duke, not me," Crystal stated. "I'm with you on that one. If he called me, I would hit that block feature so fast his head would spin."

"We're on the same page there," Abi agreed. People could be real jerks. She thought about what Grayson had said when she told him about her dad. His reaction restored her hope in humanity.

But then Grayson was just good. His list of positive qualities grew by the minute.

"I better go," Crystal said. "Wade just walked into the lobby with lunch."

Food. Abi's stomach must've heard because it picked that moment to growl. "Eat. Rest. Take care of yourself." As stressed as Abi was by the situation, the case was a distraction. Crystal was in the thick of it. Caregiver stress was real.

"Which one of us is the big sister here?" Crystal teased. The words were meant to be playful but the undertone to her voice spoke volumes. Abi's sister was exhausted. "I'm supposed to be looking out for you. Remember?"

"I'll keep that in mind," Abi teased back. Her heart wasn't in the lightheartedness, and neither was Crystal's, but they were paddling hard, trying not to get sucked under by the gravity of their grandparents' long-term health concerns.

"I'll talk to you soon," Crystal said before exchanging goodbyes and ending the call.

"I couldn't help but overhear the conversation," Grayson said after a couple of minutes ticked by.

"I am right here," she responded with a small smile. It faded too quickly.

"I'm an only child," Grayson started. "The product of divorced parents who couldn't agree the sky was blue let alone any decision that had to do with me. My mom got so frustrated that she gave up fighting my dad. She gave him custody and I only saw her summers and holidays. She put on a brave face, but I could tell she never quite recovered from the divorce. It wasn't until years later that she told her side of the story. She was in her sophomore year of college when she got pregnant with me. She and my dad decided she would quit school to be a stay-at-home mom. It was harder than she realized. She felt isolated. They didn't have money while he finished school so she did everything she could to help. Nothing she tried took off, so she gave up and decided to be the best wife and mother. She put her heart and soul into being the 'model' wife and never felt so alone in her life. When she caught Dad cheating with the community college student they'd hired to babysit me for their date nights, Mom broke down. She put all her energy into fighting him for custody, which put her in the hole. Dad ended up marrying and divorcing my babysitter. They lasted a couple of years until she talked about expanding their family. For Dad, one kid was more than enough."

She noticed his grip tightened on the steering wheel when he mentioned his father.

"The reason I'm telling you this is because I just got to witness family when it works," he said, his voice had a raspy edge to it like a cloud filled with emotion that was about to burst into a rain shower. "Believe me when I say that I'm taking notes because that's the kind of unconditional love and support that I want for Collin."

Abi had to fight to hold back tears that were like racehorses lined up at the starting gate on race day.

Abi wasn't a crier.

And yet, tears spilled out anyway, streaking her cheeks.

"I'm sorry if I said something to upset you," Grayson immediately chimed in.

"That was the most beautiful compliment that I could ever receive," she said. "I guess I'm not used to it."

"You should be, Abi. You deserve the world."

Could Grayson give it to her when he seemed determined to move on with his life? Would he shut her out in the process?

# Chapter Sixteen

Grayson reached across the console and took Abi's hand in his. One-handed steering was no problem on this stretch of highway, and that was easily accomplished with his left hand. The only concern was fighting the wind gusts. With a low-profile vehicle that was less of a problem. He'd done this stretch in a van once while interviewing a prisoner who was being transferred. That trip had him reaching for the van walls, praying they wouldn't end up in a death roll.

"The only gift of not having parents was having each other and our grandparents," Abi said.

"That makes me wonder who Collin has other than me," Grayson said.

"You're an amazing father, Grayson," she pointed out. "You're being too hard on yourself."

"Maybe," he conceded, not yet ready to agree.

"Look at Aiden," she continued. "That kid has it bad. He'd said his lawyer parents didn't care about him. They were more concerned with keeping him above the law than meeting his needs. When you're not thinking about this case, your mind is always with your son. The fact that you think about him at all in terms of his needs beats both of our fathers."

"I can't argue there," he said.

"Plus, you have us now too," she stated with a hitch in her voice. "We're friends, remember?"

The word *friends* was wholly inadequate to describe the mix of emotion swirling around in his chest like a dust storm. But it was a place to start.

"Your friendship means the world, Abi." He gave her hand a little squeeze, ignoring the electrical impulses shooting up his arm seeking an outlet as they exploded in his chest. He cracked a smile. He couldn't help it. The effect Abi had on him was something out of this world. As much as he wanted to hang on to it and see where it could go, he knew their time together would end. Then what? The occasional phone call? He was lousy at texting and even worse at keeping in touch if someone wasn't sitting right in front of him.

Could he change his ways for Abi?

Because she would be worth trying for.

AUSTIN TRAFFIC WAS a beast, as usual. While Grayson met up with his contact to hand off evidence from the crime scene, Abi figured this was as good a time as any to make a courtesy call to the sheriff before filing her report. She checked to see if the addendum had been filed by Deputy Carlson and found that it had.

"Sheriff Benton," he said, answering on the first ring.

Abi needed to feel him out first before dropping the bombs about his deputy. "Sheriff, Marshal Remington here."

"Yes, ma'am," he said, not sounding one bit the wiser about what went down at the garage. "How can I help you?"

"I visited the crime scene this morning and noticed

there were many items left off Deputy Carlson's report," she said, throwing out the first piece of bait to fish around for what he knew.

"Carlson informed me that he realized he'd left important evidence off the initial report," Sheriff Benton said, an air of question marks in his tone as if to say, *why are you telling me this*.

"Sir, did he mention why he'd had the change of heart about what to include in the list?" she continued, not ready to give up her hand.

"Said he missed cataloging a few important items in the heat of the moment but circled back to make sure he'd done a good job since he knew this was an important case," the sheriff responded.

"He didn't mention running into me and Agent Chisolm?"

"No, ma'am. He did not."

"Or the fact that we were the ones who noticed the missing items?" she continued.

"No, ma'am." Now the sheriff sounded frustrated. "I apologize for my deputy's actions. He's not a bad pers—"

"I'm guessing he also didn't mention that one of the pieces of evidence he forgot to mention was an old convertible," she said, cutting him off. Deputy Carlson wasn't a good person. At a minimum, he was lazy.

"No, ma'am."

"I'm sure you're aware of the auto repair shop owner, who shares the last name Carlson," she said.

"I am," Sheriff Benton said as it seemed to dawn on him where she was going with this.

"Are you further aware of how much money can be made from selling rare automobile parts piece by piece or restoring an old vehicle?" she pressed.

The line went dead quiet.

"I'm calling to inform you because I didn't want to surprise you with the report I'm about to write up," she explained. "If Deputy Carlson had been honest with you about what happened this morning, I'd have more confidence he was trying to do the right thing."

Again, the line was quiet.

Then came, "This report you said you were writing up, will it contain all the information you just shared with me?"

"Yes, sir. It will."

"All right then," the sheriff said. "I'll place Deputy Carlson on administrative leave pending an investigation into this and past cases." He issued a sharp sigh. "Carlson has been requesting to work auto thefts for years."

"There's a pattern," she said.

"I appreciate your courtesy in calling before you filed the report," Sheriff Benton said. The man came across as trying to do a good job. Did he hire relatives? Yes. One of whom was fencing parts under the sheriff's nose? Yes. Was he too trusting? Probably.

He could have blown up at her or tried to flip the script. Instead, he owned up to the possibility he had a problem on his staff, and that was always a good sign.

"No problem," Abi responded. "You deserve a heads-up before this goes into the system."

"I'll take care of Deputy Carlson on my end," he committed. "He'll be handing over his badge and weapon in a matter of minutes."

"Just so you're aware, I could be filing sexual harassment charges on the deputy," she stated.

"My wife will string him up by his ears when she hears this," Sheriff Benton promised.

"I'll add a few of his remarks to the report and leave you to handle it how you deem necessary," she stated.

"After this conversation, I'll put him through the firing process and let the committee decide if criminal charges apply," the sheriff said. "Conduct unbecoming a law enforcement officer while involved with a cooperative agency is unprofessional. Deputy Carlson's actions won't be tolerated by anyone in this administration."

"I have every confidence you'll take appropriate action, sir."

They exchanged goodbyes before ending the call. Abi had a good read on the sheriff. Deputy Carlson was taking advantage of working for a relative. Distant cousin on his wife's side? Either way, judgment day was on the horizon for the deputy. She wondered how much more the sheriff would find once the committee started digging into Carlson's work.

Abi hit Send on the report at the exact moment Grayson showed up holding two coffees in his hands. She hit the button to roll down the window and took them both. The man was part angel.

He claimed the driver's seat. Before he started the engine, she gave him the quick and dirty rundown on her conversation with the sheriff and the fact she'd just sent the report.

"I believe Sheriff Benton isn't involved in Carlson's dealings," she said.

Grayson nodded after taking a sip of fresh brew. "Same here."

Abi was reassured by the fact she and Grayson were on the same page. His years of experience outnumbered hers by a decade. It gave her confidence she was on the right track with her career.

Or were they just twin flames?

Abi squashed the thought.

"I'd like to meet Collin," she surprised herself in saying as Grayson started the engine.

He sat there for a long moment, engine idling, not responding.

Meanwhile, Abi's heart pounded a drum solo inside her rib cage.

"I think Collin would like that very much," he finally said, causing her to release the breath she'd been holding. "Besides, you know more about me and my family than anyone else. You might as well take a front-row seat to our chaos." He cracked a smile that could melt Texas roads during a February ice storm.

"We might be close-knit, but I think you'll find just as much havoc in my family," she said with a laugh.

"Challenge accepted," he quipped.

"Good," she said. "Because I'd also very much like the rest of my family to meet you."

Abi held her breath again, waiting for a response.

"I'd like that," Grayson said without hesitation this time.

"Good," she said. "It's settled."

"I know your family is going through a tough time with your grandparents," he interjected, killing the light mood. Was he about to let her down softly? "So, no rush on trying to schedule any get-togethers."

Yep. The air was being let out of the balloon. She didn't want to give herself away as to just how deflated the comment made her feel. "Yeah, sure. Of course. Nothing in the immediate future. We do have a lot on our plates."

"First things first," he said. "Let's find and arrest this bastard so we can get you home."

Why did Abi feel a wall come up between them when they'd been doing nothing but using a sledgehammer against one all day?

Had she been reading too much into their conversations? Because she felt an intimacy with Grayson that she'd never known with anyone else.

He was right about one thing, though. It was time to shift all focus to the investigation now that they were in Austin, fed and caffeinated themselves.

"What do I owe you for this?" she asked, holding up her latte.

"Nothing," he said, his tone steady and calm like he hadn't just jammed a safety pin in her balloon. "It's on the house."

"Well, I'm keeping a running total because I don't want to owe you anything once this case wraps up," she stated. "Next one is on me."

Grayson was quiet for a long moment. Contemplating?

She hoped he got the message because she wasn't kidding. Abi survived fine on her own. She didn't need anyone else's charity.

Period.

GRAYSON HAD NO idea what had just happened to shift the air in the cab of his sedan, but he made a mental note to circle back and ask about it later. "Either our perp plans to strike in Austin next or he is starting to save clippings of his notoriety."

"Agreed," came the one-word response.

"There are more colleges than UT in Austin," he said.

"The parties should cross over," she stated. "I've heard of kids driving down from Waco to attend a party at UT."

"Right," he said. "There will be a lot of ground to cover."

"I sent a text to Julie, asking her to alert administrations of an increased threat," she said. Her voice held no emotion when she spoke now, save for the cold chill to it. She was in all-business mode. It was probably good for the case even though he missed the warmth that had been radiating from her a few minutes ago. Being near Abi when she smiled was like stepping into the sun. If the sun was also sexy as hell.

"Here's hoping college kids listen," he said.

"She responded that UT promised to send an emergency alert text to its students about increased threats at parties," she said. "If I had to guess, he will target UT based on the evidence we have so far."

He didn't point out the fact Carlson's shoddy work could have caused them to lose pieces of evidence that could point them in a new direction. The article was their best bet, though.

"Are you surprised the perp didn't circle back to retrieve his belongings?" Abi asked.

"Not really," he said. "The area was too hot. I believe he will circle back at some point, though."

"It might be a good idea to see if the sheriff can reach out to the property owners to see if he can place a camera there," she stated.

"Can't hurt," he said.

Abi picked up her cell and tapped the screen before sending a text. "Done." She leaned her head back and pinched the bridge of her nose. "Now what else can we do to prevent this bastard from being successful with his next target?"

"Austin PD is on alert, I'm assuming," he said.

"Julie would have thought to give them a heads-up," Abi informed him.

"With their cooperation along with campus security and university administration, we have a lot of eyes and ears in Austin."

Was it enough?

# Chapter Seventeen

"Do you want to grab an early dinner?"

Abi wasn't in the mood to spend more time with the gorgeous, kind agent when she needed a nap. Plus, separation from Grayson would help her hit the reset button on her attraction. They had hours to kill before parties started rocking and rolling. All the other agencies had been notified of the heightened risk. And there wasn't much else they could do at this point. Besides, she could use the break before emotion tried to overtake logic again and convince her they had some kind of future together beyond casual friendship. "No, thanks. I'll just order room service." She held her room key in her hand as they stood at the elevator bank.

A flash of defeat crossed Grayson's features before he pulled it together and brought back his neutral expression. "I should check in at home. Make sure all is well with Collin and the babysitter." He hit the button to call the elevator. They were on the same floor with adjoining rooms. Abi intended to keep all doors locked this time.

"What time should we meet up again?" she asked as the elevator dinged.

The doors opened and they stepped inside.

"How does eight o'clock sound?" he asked as she

pushed the button to the seventh floor. The hotel was rated four stars. The check-in person was appropriately accommodating. And the beds were hailed as the most comfortable in downtown Austin. Somehow, she doubted that was true, but a soft bed and warm covers were all she needed at this point.

"Good for me," she responded.

The seventh floor arrived smoothly. She got out first and headed to room number 714. Grayson stood in front of 712, his room, long enough to indicate he was lingering for a reason. Did he have something to say?

Abi wasn't in the right frame of mind to discuss anything but the case right now. She sure as hell didn't need him to "let her down easy" if that was what he was winding up to say.

In a preempt, she flashed the hotel card key at the receiving box and immediately stepped inside without so much as a glance in Grayson's direction. There was no need to punish herself by looking at him and she sure as hell didn't need him to feel sorry for her.

Standing on the other side of her door after closing it, she could have sworn she heard his footsteps in the hallway, heading toward her room. Rather than go down that path, she headed to the bathroom, stripped and grabbed a quick shower. She might be facing a long night ahead and had no idea when she'd have this opportunity again. Despite being early on in her career by comparison, she'd learned to take advantage of these moments.

After showering, she threw on a hotel bathrobe, closed the blackout curtains and set an alarm. Three hours should be enough sleep to keep her going and fresh all night if needed. And then Abi climbed underneath the covers and closed her eyes.

GRAYSON WAS IN new territory. He'd never once in his career fallen for a coworker or task force member. Abi might have said nice things about Collin, but she'd been clear about not liking young children. Grayson couldn't date someone who couldn't accept Collin. The relationship wouldn't go anywhere, and he was long past casual flings.

He thought she was being polite by inviting him and Collin to meet her family, but the response he'd gotten from her when he tried to let her off easy caught him off guard. She'd seemed genuinely hurt.

And now?

She didn't want to be in the same room with him. Sleeping in the same bed with her last night had been the most intimate he'd been with someone since Michelle. And their clothes had stayed on the entire night. It had been enough to have Abi curled around him. Not having sex had never been sexier.

Abi was sexy. Intelligence was sexy. Strength was sexy. She had those traits in spades and even more than he cared to count. The list would be too long.

There was another bigger problem with their friendship. He didn't want to be friends with Abi. He wanted more and he picked up on the fact she did too. Except their lives were moving in different directions and he had a kid. Their schedules could be overcome with the right strategy. The kid was nonnegotiable.

Plus, what if Collin met Abi and liked her? What then? She would be a temporary fixture in Collin's life, which couldn't be good for him. If Abi met Collin, it should be as Grayson's girlfriend.

*Hold on there.* Was this a case of putting the cart before the horse?

In order for Abi to become Grayson's girlfriend she

would have to reciprocate his feelings. Their mutual attraction couldn't be denied. Making the decision to act on that attraction was a different ball game.

That was tricky, given their lives and careers.

Abi was a field agent who loved her job. Grayson was on the verge of leaving the Bureau after taking a desk jockey position for a while until he figured out his next move. He was about to devote himself to dad duty. Not exactly the recipe for starting a new relationship with someone who didn't live in the same city, was married to her job, and didn't like kids.

If he'd met Abi before Michelle, he might have had a different life and a possibility to be in a relationship with her. Even through the pain of losing his wife, he couldn't regret Collin. That kid was an angel walking on earth. Or, should he say, an angel playing with Thor and Iron Man figurines.

Grayson's heart said Abi would fall in love with Collin and change her mind about kids, but logic warned him against it. And the question ended up being: how much was Grayson willing to risk to find out?

Because Grayson could handle the pain of loving and losing but would it break Collin?

Slouched in the chair next to the window, he was jerked out of his reverie when his cell buzzed. Abi?

He fished it out of his pocket and checked the screen. Panic gripped him when he saw Martha's name.

"Everything okay?" he immediately asked. Part of the curse of losing the woman he'd loved in tragic fashion meant he was always waiting for another shoe to drop.

"Collin has a tiny fever," Martha explained. Her calm voice should settle his nerves but that wasn't the way the curse worked. It took a nugget of information and worked it in the back of his mind for hours, sometimes days, until torturing him with several worst-case scenarios.

When he was with Abi, however, the curse held at bay, and he could finally let his guard down and breathe.

How was that for doubling down on the curse? You get to find a woman you could truly love but she won't like kids.

"What qualifies as tiny?" Grayson immediately asked.

"It's a hundred and one," she replied, the information causing Grayson's pulse to rise.

"How long has this been going on?" Grayson fired. *The Wiggles* sounded in the background. If someone had told a young Grayson he would be able to sing half their songs before his thirty-eighth birthday, he would have laughed.

"I called the minute it started," Martha calmly replied. "He's right here on my lap."

Of the two of them, Martha was probably the better choice to take care of Collin while he was sick. But it wrecked Grayson to be away from his kid when he needed him most. It took a moment like this to confirm what Grayson already knew…his time in the field was up.

Part of him was ready to wrap up this case for more than just the obvious reason, to get the murdering bastard off the street. It was crystal clear to him now that he needed to be available for his boy. The other part of him wasn't ready to wrap up his time with Abi. That was the selfish part—the part that wanted to consider a future with her once this case was over.

Unrealistic as it might be, his heart had spoken.

"Did you call Dr. Frank?" Grayson asked.

"No reason to yet," Martha said. "I'll keep monitoring him, though. I gave him medicine, which should start working in the next ten minutes or so. If it doesn't bring the fever down, I'll give the pediatrician's office a call and see where we are. It's after hours, so he'll probably ask me if I've given Collin anything for the fever before he sends us to be looked at."

Martha was covering all the bases. She had far more experience at keeping kids alive than Grayson. He trusted her judgment and experience.

And yet, everything inside him wanted to rush home right now and see that Collin was okay with his own eyes. Since he would probably only stress his son out in the process, he decided it was best to let Martha handle the situation.

The other issue pressing hard on him at the moment was the need to save a life. If he didn't put 100 percent of his focus on the case, someone could die tonight.

The slap of reality made his next move crystal clear.

"Thank you for calling, Martha," Grayson said, meaning every word. "I have no idea if I tell you how much you mean to this family nearly enough, but we're damn lucky to have you."

"It's a beautiful family you have here, Grayson," she said, and he could almost feel her smiling in those words. "I'm the lucky one."

"Not sure about that," he said, thinking he would bring home a box of those doughnuts she loved when he could put this case behind him. "This is going to be my last case in the field."

"Oh?"

"I'm missing too much at home," he said. "Which means I'll probably need you even more in the near future but I'm certain desk work is the right move for me while Collin is still young."

"You love him, Grayson," she reminded in the grandmotherly tone that wrapped you in a hug. "Either way, he's a lucky boy."

"You'll stick around and show me the ropes, right? Because I wouldn't have gotten through these past years without you."

"I'm always next door," Martha said. "And I have no plans to go anywhere." She hesitated, which was uncharacteristic of her.

"Are you okay?" he asked.

"Yes, fine," she said a little too quickly. Something was up but he wouldn't force her to talk about it before she was ready.

"Once I get home, maybe we can go out to breakfast or coffee after dropping Collin off at preschool," he said, offering her an option to talk about whatever was on her mind.

"I'd like that," she said, sounding satisfied. "In the meantime, I'll keep you posted on Collin."

"Maybe the medicine will bring down his temperature," Grayson said.

"I hope so," she said. "He's still taking sips from his juice box. That'll help keep him hydrated."

Martha had things under control. She would alert him if the fever persisted. Still, the dark cloud returned.

"Sounds good," he said, not feeling one bit of those words.

They ended the call, and he made a cup of coffee. He missed the days when hotels had small pots that made two cups at a time. Everything changed. Change was in the air for him too.

And he hoped he hadn't just cursed the case by announcing to Martha that it would be his last.

ABI TOSSED AND turned for three hours. Instead of getting out of bed rested, she had to drag herself out from underneath the covers. *Coffee.*

Logic said food first, so she grabbed the room service menu, ordered a quinoa bowl with tuna, and then made a cup of fresh brew. It was quiet next door but then she'd placed a towel underneath the connecting doors to keep out light before going to bed a while ago.

Food arrived five minutes after she freshened up and got dressed. The coffee was cold by the time she picked up the cup, so she placed a few ice cubes inside and downed it like a shot anyway. It was a means to an end at this point.

The meal was decent, the room nice, but it was time to get dressed and out onto the party scene. Abi made certain to put on her Kevlar vest underneath her button-down shirt. Next came her shoulder holster before her blazer.

To keep hair off her face, she pulled hers into a low bun and then used just enough makeup to keep her from looking like the walking dead.

It was strange how much she missed being with Grayson, considering she barely knew the man. But did she barely know him? Because part of her felt like they'd known each other her whole life. Twin flames?

She was beginning to believe it was possible.

"Hey," Grayson said after joining her at the elevator bank.

"Did you sleep?" she asked, searching for something neutral to say.

"Not much. You?"

"I got to power down," she admitted. "But no real sleep."

"We can stop off for coffee since we'll be patrolling until we see something or receive word."

"Sounds good," she said. They were searching for a needle in a haystack.

Two cups of coffee and three hours later, they sat downtown with no idea of where to go next and no solid leads. The tip line was getting plenty of action, but nothing was panning out so far.

Frustration ate away at Abi as they navigated the one-way streets downtown.

A phone call had Grayson pulling over. After a few *uh-huhs* and *I-sees*, he locked gazes. "My son's fever has spiked. I don't live that far from here. I can drop you off anywhere you want but I have to check on him." The panic in his voice got her heart racing too.

"Don't let me hold you up," she said without hesitation. "Let's go."

Not two seconds later, they were racing toward his home.

## Chapter Eighteen

"Everything okay?" Abi asked once Grayson met her in the living room where she stood at the door.

"It's late and there isn't anything else we can do to-night," Grayson said to Abi. "I can't leave until I make sure Collin's fever is down in the morning. It's the only way I'll be able to focus on the case."

"Makes sense. I can grab a motel room nearby," she said, feeling more at home the minute she stepped into his house than in her own townhouse. The feeling should scare her, but she was so damn tired of fighting it. So she didn't.

"There's a guest room," he quickly stated. "You might be more comfortable here than at a random motel."

"Lead me to it," she said.

"I'll grab your bag from the car first," he said with a spark in his eyes that was another big red-flag type warn-ing signal. Again, she was too tired to struggle against the current washing over her and through her, pulling her toward the man she knew better than to fall in love with. Abi cracked a smile. Since when did her stubborn heart listen to logic?

Could she compete with a ghost?

Grayson disappeared into the garage, returning a few moments later as she studied the pictures of Michelle.

Surprisingly, Abi felt didn't feel a shred of jealousy as she looked at the smiling woman who seemed so happy. Instead, she felt sorry for Collin, who would never know his mother.

"It's good that you have pictures of her around," Abi stated.

"Really?" Grayson asked. "Because I almost took them down. They broke my heart to look at them in those first few months. Hell, years."

"It's good for Collin to see how happy his mother was," she pointed out. "We never talked about my mom, and I always wondered what she was like." It occurred to her that she might never be able to ask her grandparents now.

"You didn't ask?"

"No," she said. "Somewhere in the back of my mind, I thought my grandparents might be offended in some way if I asked about her. Like I was saying they weren't enough."

"I never thought about it in those terms," Grayson said after a thoughtful pause.

"You should tell Collin stories about her now while he's young," she said. "It'll make it easier for him to ask questions later. Otherwise, he might get it in his head the subject is taboo, like I did."

Grayson stood so close that his spicy male scent filled her senses. Before she got lost in him, she took her bag so she could head into the guest quarters. Unfortunately, their fingers grazed during the transfer. Abi was unprepared for the jolt of electricity that coursed through her. It was a force. One that made the earth tilt on its axis and made her fight the urge to lean toward him, push up to her tiptoes and kiss him.

The air crackled with electricity in between them, heating the room several degrees.

Abi had to get away or risk crossing a professional line—a line that she refused to cross with anyone. Even Grayson.

"I...um...have to...bathroom." She shook her head in an attempt to shake off the fog that was all Grayson. "That's not right...shower."

With that, she pulled on every last ounce of strength she had. Like a planet pulling out of its orbit, with effort, she managed to drum up enough power to walk away.

Since Abi had never felt anything that came close with anyone else, she could only imagine what a kiss would feel like. Would it catch her on fire? Consume her? Her lips burned to explore his. An ache the size of a canyon formed in her chest for this man.

After placing her bag inside the guest room, she immediately hit the shower. As much as she tried to refocus her attention, it was impossible. So she stopped fighting that too. There was power in surrender.

When it came to Grayson, she had no choice but to give in to her feelings. While they worked a case together, however, she refused to act on them.

Shower. Bed. Sleep.

Those three things reset just about anything in Abi's experience.

THE SUN PEEKED through the slats of the mini blinds, waking Abi after a deep sleep. She glanced at the clock and realized she'd gotten a solid seven hours. Not bad during the heat of a case.

After freshening up in the bathroom and then throwing on borrowed sweats and sweatshirt, she moved toward the kitchen in search of food and caffeine, not necessarily in that order.

Sounds coming from the living room stopped her cold in the hallway. Cartoons?

Was that a good sign Collin was feeling better?

Abi was way out of her league when it came to kiddos. Was that the curse of being the youngest of the family? She'd grown up around foals but no human kids younger than her. How different could they be?

Did she just compare babies to foals? Yep. Definitely not winning this morning.

To get to the kitchen, Abi had to cross the living room. The sudden urge to sneak out a window, circle the house and come in through the back door struck. Okay, now she was really losing it. *It's just a kid, Abi. A human. How hard can it be to say hello and then get breakfast?*

Taking in a breath to fortify herself, Abi squared her shoulders and marched toward the living room. All she had to do was cross over to the kitchen without making eye contact and she'd be fine. While in the office, she walked with purpose so no one would talk to her. The same strategy could work now, right?

Two steps into the living room and she froze.

"Are you my daddy's friend?" the little boy with glasses too big for his angelic face asked.

"That's right," she confirmed. "You must be Collin." Why was her pulse racing like she'd just sprinted across a football field chasing a perp? *Calm down, Abi. It's just a kid.*

Collin's wide smile cracked what was left of her heart in two.

"Want to watch *Iron Man* with me?" he practically beamed.

"Yes," she said before thinking her answer through. The thought of disappointing that face shredded her. No way could she have refused.

So she sat down next to him on the carpet flooring and crisscrossed her legs. He immediately climbed onto her lap. It was a good thing the kid's back was to her so he didn't see her reaction. Her jaw dropped open as every muscle in her body tensed. How could he become comfortable with her this quick? Did she have a hidden talent? Child whisperer?

*Whoa, there! Don't be too pleased with yourself. You stayed one night, not forever. The kid climbed in your lap. He didn't call you Mommy.*

One thing was abundantly clear. The kid had wriggled his way into Abi's heart in a matter of minutes.

"What's your name?" Collin asked.

"Abi," she supplied.

"How old are you?" he asked, eyes glued to the show even though his attention seemed to be split between her and the TV.

Meanwhile, Abi—ever astute being that she was—couldn't for the life of her figure out what to do with her hands. Should she hug him? No. That didn't sound right.

Leaning back, she put her flat palms on the carpet to brace herself. The kid, however, made himself right at home. He seemed unbothered by physical contact.

She could do this. She could be easy-breezy. No problem.

"I'm twenty-eight years old," she said.

"Wow," Collin responded. "I'm this many." He held up four fingers. "My birthday's in three weeks." He proudly extended fingers and thumb. "I'll be this many."

"Five?" she asked, unsure what to say to that. "Do you go to school?"

"I'm sick," Collin said, not sounding terribly disappointed about missing school.

"Do you like school?" she asked, figuring she might as well throw herself into the conversation.

"Not really," he said. She could hear a frown in his voice.

"Why not?" she asked. "Don't you like the teacher?"

"Ms. Brown is nice." Collin perked up.

"What do you do in school?" she continued.

"Learn stuff," he answered.

She might as well go all-in at this point. "Don't you like to learn stuff?"

He craned his neck around to face her. "Learning makes me smart."

"Then, why don't you like school?"

He shrugged.

The reason dawned on her. "Do you have friends?"

"Michael is my best friend," Collin supplied. "Kids say mean things to him too."

Suddenly, Abi was right back in grade school, being picked on for wearing glasses. "Kids used to say mean things to me because I wore glasses."

"But you're pretty," Collin said like it was as obvious as the nose on her face.

"Mean kids say mean things to everyone," she said. "And it's okay to stick up for yourself when they do or tell the teacher."

"Teacher says we're not supposed to be tattle tales," Collin said.

Grayson needed to have a discussion with Ms. Brown or move Collin to a preschool that didn't put up with bullying. How Ms. Brown could not defend a sweet kid like Collin was beyond her.

"There's tattling to get someone in trouble and then there's another thing called letting a teacher know when someone is acting bad," Abi said.

Collin cocked his head to one side. His face scrunched in serious thought.

"The teacher wants to know when someone is acting bad," Abi continued, hoping that clarified things. "So she can help them act better."

"Will they get in trouble?" he asked.

"Sometimes," Abi said. "Other times, they'll be sent over to say they are sorry."

"Rupert would never do that," Collin exclaimed, shaking his head in the process.

At least they had a name. She could tell Grayson so he could reach out to Rupert's parents. Maybe stop by on the way to work this morning. Or they could swing by and have a conversation with Ms. Brown.

Either way, the bullying needed to stop.

"Hold on a second," Abi said. She picked Collin up and set him down next to her before getting up. "I'll be right back."

She popped out her contacts and then put her glasses on.

When she returned to the living room, Collin's face lit up. He clapped and beamed at her.

"You have glasses too?" It was more excited statement than question.

"That's right," she said. "And I think yours are pretty cool."

She sat down and he immediately crawled in her lap again.

He twisted half his body around when he looked up at her this time. "Can you be my new Mommy?"

If words were bullets, those were the equivalent of being sprayed with an AR-15s.

"Hey," Grayson said from the kitchen before she could find the words to come up with an answer. His voice cracked on the word, which gave the impression he'd been standing there long enough to hear the question that had rocked Abi's world.

Was it strange that she'd only known the kid for a matter of minutes but would jump at the chance to be his Mommy? Abi! Someone who never wanted the white picket fence or the 2.5 kids running around. Abi! Who never saw herself in a Cinderella ball gown wedding dress or any other white dress for that matter. Abi! Who used to think of kids as not much more than an annoyance on airplanes.

Boy, hadn't she been dead wrong. The crying might not be a kid's best moment but sitting on a living room floor with one on her lap made her wonder if getting moments like these made all the others worth it.

Much to her surprise, Collin didn't jump up and run to his dad.

Grayson walked into the living room. His thick wet hair stuck up at odd angles, making him surprisingly more handsome. He had that fresh-from-the shower look, which had never looked so good on any other human. He wore pajama bottoms and a cotton T-shirt. Those had never looked sexier on a man either. Then again, Grayson's body was made for sinning.

"Hey, buddy," Grayson said. "How about that breakfast I promised you?"

Collin looked up at Abi with big blue eyes. "Will you stay?"

"For breakfast?" she asked with a smile. "Of course, I will."

The kid's smile melted what was left of her resolve as he let out a little yelp. He scrambled to his feet and then took hold of Grayson's hand.

Her heart couldn't take much more of this. Abi fought the urge to come up with an escape plan. Maybe all this was telling her was that she might be ready to open her life to someone. That having someone to go home to, to share her life with wasn't such an awful thing.

Of course, it would have to be the right person. Someone like Grayson. Now that she had the blueprint, it shouldn't be hard to find. Right?

Abi's heart said Grayson was one of a kind. The mold was broken after him. Hell's bells.

If she couldn't find another Grayson, there was no way she could settle for less now that she knew exactly what she was looking for.

Was being alone the worst thing? It had never seemed so in the past. Why now?

The answer came quickly. Life was short. She worked a dangerous job. And even if she didn't, there were no guarantees. The thought of dying without ever being loved suddenly sounded like the loneliest fate. The ache in her chest expanded.

Was there a slight chance Grayson felt the same way? If so, could she be brave enough to ask?

# Chapter Nineteen

Grayson's heart nearly exploded out of his chest when he walked into the kitchen and heard his son ask Abi to be his Mommy. Did his son feel a tremendous void in the space where a mother's love would be?

Collin had to or he wouldn't have asked. And Grayson had never felt so inadequate or underprepared.

Seeing his son insist Abi sit next to him at the table warmed Grayson's heart. But the fact she was temporary in Collin's life needed to be kept in focus.

"Where do you live?" Collin asked as Grayson set down a bowl of cereal along with a banana. At least Collin's fever was down. Martha would be over in half an hour and Grayson could return to work with Abi.

"Far away but I grew up on a horse ranch about two hours from here," Abi supplied.

"What do you like for breakfast?" Grayson asked her. "I have hardboiled eggs, ham and a few tomatoes."

"Sounds perfect to me," she said.

Out of the blue, Collin exclaimed, "I like her." For a kid that had been sick with fever last night, he beamed today. Abi probably had something to do with it, but Grayson was relieved his son was feeling better. Kids bounced back at a surprising rate. Meanwhile, Grayson's joints liked to remind him of his age first thing when he got out of bed. He had to stretch before firing off a few pushups to get the blood pumping. He couldn't remember where he'd picked up the saying *Motion is lotion,* but it was true. His body was like the Tin Man from *The Wizard of Oz.*

After putting together twin plates, he made a pot of coffee.

"Can I help with anything?" Abi asked.

"You want to grab the plates?" Grayson responded as he filled two mugs.

She joined him in the kitchen, moved beside him so close he could smell the lavender bodywash from the guest bathroom. It had never smelled so good.

Shoulder to shoulder, she whispered, "I got a name of the ringleader at preschool who is bullying Collin. The little twerp's name is Rupert. Should we stop by the pre-school and have a chat with Ms. Brown or go directly to the brat's parents?"

"You got a name?" Grayson asked. Collin never said any one individual was responsible. He always spoke generically.

"Sure did," Abi said, seemingly not realizing how monumental that felt to Grayson.

"Why doesn't he say anything to the teacher?" Grayson asked, figuring she might not know but it didn't hurt to go for broke.

"Doesn't want to be a narc," she stated.

"Do you think Ms. Brown will handle the situation?" Grayson asked. "Because I've been thinking of moving him to a new school."

"I can go with you if you want to set up a meeting," Abi offered. "Sometimes it helps to have an extra set of eyes and ears. A different perspective."

"You would do that?" Grayson was caught off guard with her eagerness to help.

"For Collin?" She paused. "I'd do anything legal for that kid. And it wouldn't be difficult to twist my arm to commit a misdemeanor if it got a bully off his back."

Abi grabbed the plates like nothing had just happened, twirled around and then headed back to the table. Meanwhile, the floor shifted underneath Grayson's feet. He had to grab hold of the bullnose edge of the counter to stay upright because he was floored.

"May I have some milk, Daddy?" Collin asked, bringing Grayson back to the present.

"Sure," he said, giving himself a moment to get back to reality. A mental headshake did the trick.

Grayson poured milk and balanced the cup along with a pair of mugs in his hands before setting them down on the table. Collin was right, though, Abi was amazing. Could his heart survive losing her once this case was closed?

ABI POLISHED OFF breakfast along with a cup of coffee in record time. She was always famished after a good night's sleep. There was something about this home that allowed her to relax.

"I should get dressed," she said after cleaning the dishes while Collin colored in a coloring book his dad brought to him at the end of the meal.

Since the pages were filled with Marvel superheroes and Collin was allowed to set his figurines down on the table, he reluctantly gave up watching them on television.

By the time Abi returned, fully dressed and with her bag in hand, the babysitter had arrived. The older woman sat at the table with Collin, reading while he colored.

"Hi," Abi said as she entered the room.

"You must be Abi," the older woman said. She had a kind face and a pile of gray hair on top of her head tied in a loose bun. "Collin's been talking about you nonstop."

"He's a great kid," Abi said as moisture gathered in her eyes. What was that all about? The thought of never seeing him again? And since when had she become a crier?

Abi had no idea what was happening to her but assumed it had a lot to do with her grandparents.

Collin's smile widened. How was that even possible? The kid was already grinning ear to ear.

"I'm Martha, by the way," she said, studying Abi, who suddenly felt subconscious.

"Nice to meet you, Martha." She could feel the heat in her cheeks. She hadn't done anything to be embarrassed about. It dawned on Abi that she wanted Martha to like her because Martha was important to Collin and Grayson.

"I hope that I'm not being too forward when I say it would be neat to see you around again sometime soon," Martha said with a wink.

"I'd like that a lot," Abi admitted. Her cheeks were on fire now.

"What are you two talking about?" Grayson asked as he joined them.

"You," Abi teased, winking at Collin.

"Ms. Brown says you're not s'posed to tell a lie," Collin said with so much earnestness that Abi's heart squeezed.

"Your teacher is right," Abi said, figuring a qualifier that she was only joking would confuse the kid. His innocence was endearing. "We were talking about me," she said to Grayson.

"She wants to come back, Daddy," Collin supplied.

Abi needed to be careful around those little ears that

seemed to catch everything. Were all kids like a sponge, like Collin?

Probably not. He was special. Sensitive.

"She's welcome anytime," Grayson said, his voice dropping an octave. The hitch was back.

Abi's cell buzzed. She fished it out of her handbag and checked the screen. One look at Grayson and he jumped into action.

"We have to go to work now," he said to Collin, who frowned.

"Can Abi come back with you?" Collin asked.

"We'll see," Grayson said, and Abi's heart gave a little flip.

"I'll see you soon," Abi said to the little boy.

"Promise?" Collin asked.

"Promise," she confirmed. Her answer seemed to satisfy him.

Grayson ruffled Collin's hair before planting a kiss on top of the boy's head. Abi turned away so no one could see the emotion once again gathering in her eyes. She cleared her throat, made a show of saying goodbye with a wave, and headed to the garage where the car was parked.

"Sandra Boylston didn't return to her dorm room last night, according to her roommate," Abi supplied as they reclaimed their seats and the garage door opened. "The roommate's name is Chloe Sharp. Sandra fits the description that Reprehensible targets. Brown hair and eyes. And she always checks in with her roommate when she sleeps somewhere else. They have a pact."

"Which dorm?" he asked.

"Jester," she stated.

"What's the address of the party?" he asked.

"21st and Alamo," she supplied. "Second house on the

right." She plugged the location into her phone's map feature. "We can be there in twenty-five minutes."

"Is there a good place to meet with the roommate near the party location?" Grayson asked. "The perp likes to stay nearby. We already know that. He'll be close. Sandra will be in a two-block range, if I had to guess."

"Alamo Pocket Park would be a good place to meet," she supplied after checking the area. "I'll request a meeting there to interview the roommate." Abi tapped out the message on her phone. Within a matter of minutes, the confirmation came through. "All set. She'll head there right now with her boyfriend."

"Good, I'm glad she's not going alone," he said.

"The task force received forty-two tips last night," Abi said. "This is one of three that seemed viable. One other checked in this morning, which leaves two."

"It's eight o'clock in the morning," he pointed out before falling silent.

"You don't think…?"

"That he will kill her immediately to satisfy what he couldn't accomplish with Max?" Grayson asked. "I hope the hell not."

Abi checked the map. Eighteen minutes until they arrived but the perp would have had hours with Sandra by now.

"What about the other tip?" he asked.

"The missing person is blonde," she supplied. "Bleached, but that might not matter to our perp."

"Let me see if I can make it there in less than fifteen minutes," Grayson said, stepping harder on the gas pedal. "Put on the light and I'll go siren until we get close."

Abi did as requested.

They made it to the park in thirteen minutes. Her cell

buzzed again. She checked the screen as Grayson parked on the street.

"Three possible locations have been pinned on the map being texted over," she said. She blew up each one. "All three have boarded-up windows, are within walking distance to the party, and neighbors would be used to and possibly even unaffected by rowdy neighbors. The one I think we should hit first is here." She tilted the screen so he could see it and pointed to the one two houses down from the corner. "It's a small duplex, but this side looks abandoned."

The area was gentrifying. A couple of new build homes were sprinkled in with mostly older homes, chain-link fences and boarded-up windows. The one she wanted to investigate first had an old, dirty towel pinned over the front window. The rag looked like it had been there for twenty years at a minimum.

"Let's meet with Chloe and then we can walk over," Grayson said. "Sound good?"

"I was just about to make the same suggestion," Abi admitted. They had no idea what kind of arsenal they would be walking into with this perp, which sent all kinds of tingles up her spine. "I'm sending a text to request Austin PD check out the other location. Time is the enemy. If this bastard has Sandra, we don't know how long he'll keep her alive."

Without another word, they exited the vehicle simultaneously. A college-age-looking female sat on her boyfriend's lap on the swing. They were the only ones at the park this early in the morning.

"She had a test tomorrow," Chloe began after they identified themselves and finished perfunctory introductions. "Has," Chloe corrected, catching herself talking about her roommate in the past tense. Bags underneath her eyes and her heavy expression said this was serious. Even if Sandra wasn't taken by the perp, something bad had happened to her in Chloe's view. Her friend's concern came across as heartfelt, genuine. "We were supposed to wake up early and study together, but one of her friends talked her into going to the party."

"What time did she leave?" Abi asked, taking the lead.

"Late," Chloe said. "Probably around eleven thirty."

"Had she been drinking?" Abi continued.

Chloe hesitated.

"No one is here to make any judgment or arrest for underage drinking," Abi quickly added in case the pause had to do with Sandra's age.

"I just turned twenty-one," Chloe said. "But Sandra had picked up a bottle of wine."

"How old is Sandra?" Abi asked.

"Nineteen," Chloe stated. She might be lying about who brought the alcohol into the dorm but ferreting out the truth about who supplied the alcohol wasn't the objective right now. Those details could be sorted out by Austin PD later.

Moving on.

Sandra fit the age the perp targeted.

"We were supposed to have a girls' night in, but Sandra's friend kept texting, said her boyfriend stood her up and she didn't want to be at the party alone," Chloe supplied.

"Does this friend have a name?" Abi asked.

"Jenn," Chloe supplied. "But I don't know her last name. She's someone Sandra met in class this semester."

"How much had Sandra had to drink before she left here?" Abi asked, figuring Sandra might have already been drunk or close to it before heading out. This could also be a false alarm as Sandra might have gone home with Jenn and forgotten to text because she was too drunk, and was currently sleeping it off.

"Most of the bottle," Chloe admitted. "I have a hard time waking up early if I drink more than a glass the night before."

Could be sugarcoating her own side of the story but she wasn't showing any tells of outright lying.

They needed to wrap this interview up and head to the residence in question.

"You didn't hear from Sandra for the rest of the evening, is that correct?" Abi continued, moving toward ending the conversation.

"No, ma'am," Chloe supplied with an exacerbated look. "And she didn't return any of my texts either."

"Phone battery could have died," Abi said.

"Sandra is militant about keeping a charge," Chloe said. "Even when she'd had way too much to drink, she texts."

"Does she overdrink often?" Abi asked.

"You know how it is first year," Chloe said honestly. "First taste of freedom."

"I'll take that as a yes," Abi said.

"Sandra is no worse than any other freshman, though," Chloe felt the need to clarify. It was good to see her being protective over her friend and roommate. "But, yes, she has been known to have a few too many."

"Agent Chisolm and I appreciate your honesty, Chloe," Abi stated. Sandra might be passed out somewhere, but she had someone looking out for her.

"She would do the same for me," Chloe said. "I just hope she's okay. I probably wouldn't have even called if not for all the alerts we've been getting." Chloe's eyes watered. "She's the right height and has the right hair color." She paused as if stopping herself from crying. "It scares me."

"Sandra is lucky to have you for a roommate," Abi pointed out. "We have a lot of resources on this. We'll do our best to find her." Abi had learned a long time ago not to make promises to folks no matter how much they needed reassurance. Time would tell when it came to Sandra. If the perp had abducted her, Abi could only pray they would find her alive. "Here's my information. I'd appreciate it if you contacted me the second you hear from Sandra."

"You can find her by tracking her phone, right?" Chloe asked, accepting the contact after giving her phone number.

"We're working on it," Abi noted. It took time to get a judge to sign off on invading someone's privacy. But approval was in the works and should come down any minute.

"Thank you," Chloe said. "For taking me seriously. For looking for Sandra. For being here so fast."

"You're welcome," Abi said. "Do me a favor?"

"Yes," Chloe said.

"As tempting as it might be, don't try to find Sandra on your own," Abi said. The last thing she needed was a young person to interfere with an ongoing investigation.

Chloe put her hands up, palms out. "I swear. It's the reason I called the tip line in the first place."

"You did the right thing," Abi reassured before ending the interview.

With that, she and Grayson headed away from the park, toward the duplex.

"What did you think?" she asked him once they were out of earshot.

"Chloe was honest," he supplied. "And we're running out of time."

The hairs on the back of Abi's neck pricked. An ominous feeling hung over her like a gray cloud before a storm.

Were they off track? Or about to come face-to-face with a monster?

## Chapter Twenty

The home on the 2000 block of Alamo was a duplex three houses down from the corner. Other homes blocked the view of the park, but it was possible to see it from the backyard. The house to the left had rocks instead of grass and pots filled with indigenous plants. The home directly across the street had been torn down and rebuilt, painted in a dark hue with wood accents around the windows and door.

The neighborhood was an odd mix of old and new, with no master plan at work. The homes on both sides of the duplex were vacant. Its tree limbs tangled in overhead electric distribution wires. The front windows had makeshift coverings.

An icy chill gripped Abi's spine. This looked exactly like the kind of place she imagined Reprehensible would take a victim. The urge to barge in to save Sandra weighed heavily against the need to be safe and protect her and her partner.

Adrenaline surged through her as she drew her weapon while Grayson sent a message to inform the team they'd arrived on scene. Bursting through the door looked good in the movies but could cost Sandra her life. Plus, they needed probable cause. A hunch without cause didn't hold up in court.

Grayson made eye contact with Abi before indicating he would take the right-hand side. She nodded, then headed left. It was quarter to nine at this point. The sun was up on a partly cloudy morning. There was a chill in the air that caused her to wish she'd put on a coat instead of the blazer that normally did the trick. She wore the Kevlar vest that clearly marked her as a US marshal on the outside of her blazer.

Grayson had essentially the same vest marked with the letters FBI instead in bright yellow. There was no mistaking them for troublemakers or would-be squatters. Weapons leading the way, careful to duck underneath windows, she listened for any signs of life inside the home.

Was there any way to get a look inside without alerting the perp to their presence?

As she came around the corner in the backyard, Abi's cell buzzed. She paused long enough to check the screen.

Wrong address. Two doors down. Neighbor heard a scream. Go!

An image along with an address popped up next. Grayson got the same message because he was by her side in a heartbeat, urging her to move.

"We get there, and we go in immediately," Grayson said. "Deal?"

"I was just thinking the same thing," Abi admitted as they bolted to the address. She was a couple of steps ahead, being the faster runner.

At the front door, she could hear sounds of a struggle

inside. It was enough for probable cause. Grayson caught up, took the opposite side of the door.

The no-knock, destroy-the-door entries were not at all fun to serve. They were hazardous for everyone involved. If Abi had her druthers, she would wait for the perp to come walking outside to get supplies from the pack he would have stashed nearby. In this scenario, she would be dressed in street clothes with a backpack on, happening by as she walked down the street like she might be a grad student, and then would say something casual before catching him off guard and then cuffing the bastard.

But that wasn't an option here. Not with Sandra's life on the line. She might be dead already except that Abi suspected the perp would have fled the scene with her limp body.

Although, he would have to wait for the cover of night. Not enough time had passed for him to pull a move like that one off successfully. If this perp was anything, he was calculating. He also knew his way around college campuses, understood the party scene well enough to blend in and somehow never get caught in the background in a picture.

A quick nod from Grayson, a moment of eye contact, and then she opened the screen so he could kick the door in. The second kick blasted the old wood.

"US marshal, put your hands up where I can see 'em," Abi demanded as she took the first step inside.

The victim, who fit Sandra's description, had wild eyes as she kicked like a banshee. She was flat on the floor on her side. Her long locks in a pile next to her, hair in a bowl cut.

The perp picked up a gun and aimed as Abi stepped outside onto the porch in search of cover. The bastard fired. A bullet pinged the wood not much more than an inch from her left ear at the entrance as she and Grayson hit the deck.

The man was tall and slim, runner's build. He had a head full of brown hair that was a little too long and unkempt. His eyes spoke pure disdain and evil, mixed with panic. Eyes like those said they'd rather die than go to prison.

There was no way they could lose this bastard. Not when they were this close.

Abi called it in, requesting all available resources to the 2000 block of Alamo. She gave the description of the killer: five feet ten inches, thin build. In her experience, guys like that could be wiry.

And then she and Grayson exchanged glances. They didn't need words. The look spoke volumes. They weren't letting this one get away.

Abi first ran inside to Sandra, who was gagged and crying. Her first move was to remove the gag and then the bindings forcing her arms behind her back.

Sandra cried hysterically as she tried to grab hold of Abi, like someone drowning would grip a ring buoy.

"I have to go," Abi said sternly, trying to shock the young woman out of her panic. "Help is on the way."

Sandra's eyes were unfocused. She reeked of alcohol, and she was still suffering the effects of sedation. There were bruises forming on her face, along with a nasty cut above her left cheekbone.

Abi's heart cracked in half at the desperation in the nineteen-year-old's eyes. But she couldn't stay.

The crack of a bullet split the air. *Grayson?*

Abi had to peel the young woman's arms off. "Help is coming. Stay right here."

Her legs were still bound but she would likely figure out how to remove the ropes. Would she stay put?

Abi couldn't stick around to find out. Grayson had already taken off after Reprehensible, and she needed to join the chase before he disappeared again. Striking this soon after Max was the equivalent of taunting law enforcement. It was saying, *I can do this right underneath your noses and you can't catch me.*

The man was smart. She would give him that much. He was a fast runner. There was no denying it. And now, she wondered if he was also a student. It would make it easier for him to blend in.

After peeling Sandra's arms off for the third time, Abi managed to break free from the desperate young woman. "I promise someone will be here in a matter of minutes."

Leaving was hard but had to be done. By the time Abi joined the chase, heading in the direction of the gunfire, she'd long lost any hope of visuals on Grayson and the perp.

A chopper overhead belonging to Austin PD was her best bet to locate them again, so she tracked to it.

Minutes had passed while she was interacting with Sandra, precious minutes. The gunfire could have been the perp firing a wild shot. The bullet could have slammed into Grayson. The image of Collin dressed in black standing at his father's gravesite fueled her to sprint even faster.

At this point, joggers were starting their mornings. Sidewalks were filling up. Austin was a twenty-four-hour city with all the college students and young professionals fighting for space. The college had more than 50,000 students, and that was UT alone. There were roughly 2.2 million residents coming from all walks of life, descending on the metro area and making it feel like being trapped in an ant farm.

With no word from Grayson, she could only pray that meant he was still giving chase and not lying on the street somewhere bleeding out with no way to contact her.

The thought of losing Grayson now that she'd finally found a friend almost caused her knees to buckle.

Another crack of a bullet split the air.

Tears streaked Abi's cheeks as she blasted through joggers on the sidewalk, praying she could find Grayson in time.

As she glanced up at the chopper, an idea came to her. Would it work? Could she afford to take a risk?

At this point, she might as well go for broke. Abi cut across the street and headed a block over. Would the move pay off? Or backfire in her face?

GRAYSON POPPED BEHIND a tree. A bullet came flying toward him, chipping off a piece of trunk. The perp was firing wild shots—shots that were getting dangerously close to hitting their mark...*him.*

He'd lost track of Abi, and the perp was a better runner than Grayson. She would have caught up to the bastard by now.

Using the massive oak tree to put some mass in between himself and the perp had kept a bullet out of him, but the killer was far enough away to disappear at any moment. Grayson couldn't let that happen.

As soon as the opportunity presented itself, Grayson made a run for it. This stretch of sidewalk had enough trees for him to run a zigzag pattern, providing at least some barrier.

The thought of being shot today crossed his mind. The last case omen?

His first thought, of course, was Collin. What would his kid do if he had to grow up without both parents? Grayson couldn't go there. Not even hypothetically. His second thought surprised him. Because it was about Abi.

Grayson had loved Michelle and he'd lost her. He'd never thought he would find that kind of love again. Lightning didn't strike twice and finding a soul mate seemed about that likely. He'd loved Michelle. However, Abi was his twin flame—a flame that burned even brighter than anything he'd known to expect.

Now Grayson had two reasons to ensure he made it home safe and alive.

Did Abi feel the same way about him? She'd been clear about not wanting kids. Would her friendship be enough?

Nearly face-planting after tripping on a root snapped his mind out of his reverie. The mind was a funny place. It went in all kinds of directions while facing danger. Grayson didn't normally allow his to wander in critical moments, which was another reason why he knew it was time to hang up his fieldwork in favor of sitting behind a desk.

The perp's legs had to be getting tired by now. Grayson's sure as hell were. His thighs burned.

He'd expected Abi to catch up to him by now, considering the speed with which she ran. Had she taken a different route? Would she stay with the victim?

The perp was almost a full block ahead of Grayson now. The chopper overhead pulled away, banking right. Was the pilot called off the search?

Grayson didn't like that one bit. Because the other explanation was the chopper didn't have eyes on them. Stop to communicate, and Grayson could lose the perp altogether. Let this bastard slip away again and he was sure to kill again.

He couldn't allow that to happen. If this was going to be his last case in the field, he needed to stop the killings now.

Adrenaline gave him a boost of energy as his lungs clawed for air.

Pumping his arms helped him to keep on pace with the perp, who was still a block ahead. With no chopper, though, the guy could slip away.

Grayson focused on the image of Sandra locked inside that abandoned house, fighting for her life. He pumped his arms harder, closing a little bit of the gap between him and Reprehensible. At this point, he'd take the inches of gain.

The perp cut across the street, heading right. A cross street was ahead. Did he have another motorcycle stashed there?

Grayson bit back a curse. He would keep pushing until there was no point if that was the case. A motorcycle in Austin would make it even easier to blend in. The highway wasn't far. This guy chose his locations near quick getaways.

Austin traffic would work against them.

The perp disappeared around the corner.

*Not again!*

As Grayson pushed his legs as hard as they could go, he made it halfway up the block in record time. Frustration seethed because he was still a few seconds too late—he'd lost visual on the guy.

Could he stop long enough to make contact with Abi? Get a location on her?

The risk of letting the perp outdistance Grayson further stopped him from trying to contact Abi.

Where was she?

ABI MADE A sharp left, rounding the corner at the fastest pace she'd ever run. Adrenaline could be thanked for the extra boost, but also the thought of anything happening to Grayson made it unnecessary.

The second she had a clear view of the street, she saw him.

Reprehensible hopped on a motorcycle, facing the opposite direction. His face glued toward the direction in which he'd come. Grayson had to be close by because the perp had his gun aimed and ready to shoot as soon as the agent rounded the corner.

Abi stopped, hopping behind a tree. She fired a text to Grayson because she had to do something to stop him. After tucking her cell inside its case on her belt, she trained her weapon on Reprehensible. He was halfway down a short block.

A faster runner than Grayson, the perp was setting the agent up to be fired on. The perp had time, too. He sat there, heaving, as he switched hands in order to start the engine.

The motorcycle itself caught her eye. It dawned on her why no one had caught him on the scene of Max's attack. The motorcycle had a sidecar with a person inside. At least, it looked like a person. Was it, though?

As she crept up from behind, she realized the passenger in the sidecar was a life-size dummy. Everyone had been looking for a single motorcycle rider. Even a chopper would dismiss the bike with a sidecar, especially since the dummy appeared to be a real person who was strapped in. A decoy.

*Smart.*

And an almost surefire way to escape in plain sight.

Abi hoped she could get close enough to disarm the

bastard before Grayson made it around the corner. The perp fully intended to shoot.

A door opened across the street. A young woman in pajamas stepped onto her porch, and then froze when her gaze landed on the perp. Abi cursed under her breath. Because the woman's gaze then shifted to her.

Abi waved her back inside her house. She complied but not before alerting Reprehensible that someone was creeping up from behind.

He immediately turned around and fired a wild shot.

Thankfully, Abi stepped behind a tree in time. "Halt! I'm a US marshal. Drop your weapon! Put your hands in the air where I can see them."

At that moment, Grayson came racing around the corner.

Attention shifting immediately to the agent who was closest to him, Reprehensible aimed and fired.

# Chapter Twenty-One

Grayson was slammed back a step after the bullet struck him in the chest. Stunned, he dropped down to his knees. The moment of shock left him vulnerable to another shot. *Collin. Abi.*

The crack of a bullet split the air again as he dove for cover. This time, the bullet whizzed past his ear on the way down.

"I said put your hands in the air where I can see them!" Abi's demand was met with the perp turning to fire in her direction.

Was he determined to be shot and killed instead of serving time? How would justice be served if the bastard was dead?

Grayson couldn't allow it. Not as long as he had breath inside him.

The Sig Sauer P365 in his hands had a lower capacity of ten rounds. Grayson had no idea if he'd reloaded to full capacity after the attempt on Max. He'd lost count on how many rounds the bastard had fired so far.

Going at him would be taking a chance. Was it worth risking his life?

Abi moved toward the perp from behind. Was she enough of a distraction to allow Grayson to get close enough to disarm the man?

A determined criminal with nothing to lose wasn't the best guy to end a field career on, but here Grayson was. There was no going back now. His job was dangerous, but he was also a damn fine agent.

Would his skills be enough?

Not going home to Collin wasn't an option. So Grayson moved in the trees as Abi shouted and moved at a slower pace.

The motorcycle was parked in between two compact cars, providing little cover but a decent line of sight.

Reprehensible seemed to sense how close he was to losing his freedom because he started firing one after the other, narrowly missing Grayson's head with one of the wild shots.

Grayson was a car's length away when he heard the telltale click, no bullet.

Not wasting a second for the perp to reload, Grayson jumped from behind the tree and barreled into Reprehensible. The last-minute dive knocked the killer off balance. He flew off the bike as Grayson grabbed hold of his sweatshirt, landing on top of the bastard. The hard fall caused Grayson's elbow to smack concrete. Pain reverberated up his arm, exploding in his shoulder.

A flurry of desperate kicks and punches was like holding on to a tornado. Grayson took a knee where no man wanted to be hit.

"Freeze or I'll shoot," Abi said. Her voice was close enough to indicate she was standing roughly five feet away.

A glance in her direction revealed she was in an athletic stance, the business end of her service weapon pointed at the two men.

The break in concentration cost Grayson an elbow to

the throat. Arms flying every which way, trying to pin this bastard down was like trying to wrestle an alligator on crack.

The perp bucked, trying to break free of Grayson's grasp. The man must know Abi wouldn't shoot while Grayson was tangled up. She wouldn't risk shooting a fellow law enforcement agent.

Grayson doubled down on strength as he wrapped his arms around the man's torso in an attempt to pin his arms to his sides.

The move almost worked. A moment before Grayson was able to clasp his fingers together, the perp broke free. He rolled straight toward Abi, who delivered a kick hard enough to scramble the perp's brain.

It gave Grayson enough time to properly pin the bastard as a flood of footsteps arrived on the scene.

Just as Grayson felt himself losing his hold, Abi was there by his side. She helped wrangle Reprehensible's arms behind his back where an officer from Austin PD slapped cuffs on the guy's wrists.

Grayson rolled onto his back as the assailant was forced to his feet. A moment later, his legs were spread, his torso flat on the hood of a compact car, and he was being searched for any additional weapons.

But when he glanced up at Abi, his blood ran cold.

Time slowed to a stop, moving frame by frame. She mouthed two words that ripped his heart to shreds: "I'm sorry."

Abi dropped down to her knees as EMTs roared up to the scene.

And he shouted the words no law enforcement professional ever wanted to utter, "Officer down."

Blood dripped from her fingertips as she sat back on her heels, in shock.

Grayson was there to catch her before she hit her head on the pavement. "Stay with me. Look at me."

Abi's gaze fixed on him. There was blood pooled on the sidewalk. She was losing too much blood. Was she in shock?

Not two seconds later, an EMT was crouched down beside Grayson.

"What's your name, sweetheart?" the young man asked. His name tag read Charley.

Calling Abi sweetheart should have had fire coursing through her. Face pale, she nodded and then forced a word out. "Abi."

"Abi, you're going to be just fine," Charley said. "Do you hear me?"

Nothing.

"Nod if you can hear me," Charley said as he cut off her blazer from neck to end of sleeve. Blood pulsed from the base of her neck like a geyser.

Charley was on it with pads and pressure. "I need a cart here. Now!"

Grayson was no doctor, but he'd swear a bullet had hit her carotid artery. He muttered a string of curses that would make his grandmother disown him if she was still alive.

He bent down to her ear, "I can't lose you, Abi." Their "friendship" or whatever she wanted to call it was too special. Would the world be so cruel as to take away the only other woman he could see himself loving?

Correction, that he loved?

"Where are you taking her?" he asked Charley as an

oxygen mask was placed over her mouth by a second EMT. Charley maintained pressure on her neck.

"Austin General," Charley shouted as she was being wheeled away.

Grayson recalled his government-issued sedan was parked a couple of blocks from here. An officer stepped into view as Grayson turned around.

"I thought you would want to know that the victim has been recovered," the Austin PD officer stated with a look of compassion. "She's already on her way to the same hospital as Marshal Remington and is being listed in stable condition."

"Thank you," Grayson said to the man.

"We'll keep the marshal in our thoughts," he said with a solemn expression. A service vehicle pulled up lights and sirens on. "Officer Perez volunteered to give you a ride to the hospital."

Grayson nodded, thanked the officer and prayed like hell Abi would survive. The only other time he'd felt this helpless was when he'd lost Michelle.

Would history repeat itself?

ABI'S MOUTH WAS as dry as Texas dirt in August. She couldn't summon enough saliva to spit if her life depended on it. She blinked through blurry eyes. Every piece of her had dried up. The cotton taste in her mouth made her want to drink a gallon of water.

"Hey," the familiar voice that had a way of sending warmth through her said.

The next sound was chair legs scraping against tile, moving toward her. She turned her head in time to see the most gorgeous face... Grayson's.

"How do you feel?" he asked, his voice heavy with concern.

"What time is it?" she asked, trying to sit up so she could have a civil conversation. She also needed to find water before her throat cracked from dryness.

"Tomorrow," he said with a smile that caused her insides to melt.

He placed the remote that controlled the bed in her hand.

"Water?" she managed to squeak out as the bed rose until she was in a comfortable sitting position.

The curtains were almost completely closed, allowing in a sliver of sunlight.

Grayson handed her a clear supersize carafe with blue markings to indicate the water level. The carafe must make it easier on the nurses to see how much water intake each patient managed without an IV.

Abi took a few sips before leaning her head back. "Better."

"Do you want me to call for a nurse?" Grayson asked. He was still in the same clothes as yesterday.

She shook her head, wanting a few more moments with just the two of them. He had a life to get back to, so he was probably waiting for her to wake up before he headed out. "Have you been here all night?"

She figured she knew the answer but asked anyway because what she wanted to tell him meant putting her heart on the line. And he needed to know how she felt about him.

"I'm not leaving your side, Abi."

A thrill of awareness shot through her at the sincerity in his voice, combined with the way he looked at her when he said it.

"Sandra?"

Grayson took his seat again but kept a hand on her. The connection sent shivers racing up her arm while causing warmth to flood her.

"She was treated and released last night," he said. "Other than a cut on her right cheek that needed twenty-four stitches and several bruises, she is going to be fine physically."

That was a relief.

"She's being provided with a list of counseling services along with victim support group information," he continued. "Her parents arrived last night and promised to get her all the help she needed."

"That's good," she said as relief washed over her. She took a few more sips of water. "She'll need support to manage the emotional scars a horrific event like this leaves."

"The family is setting up a victims' rights fund in your name," Grayson supplied.

"Me?"

"You saved Sandra's life," he said. "You saved mine too, in more ways than one."

"It's my job," she countered. "It's what we do."

"You were amazing," he continued as she tried to not read too much into his last statement.

"Your sister was notified, by the way. She asked me to tell you that there's no change in your grandparents," he continued.

"You spoke to Crystal?"

"Yes," he confirmed. "Everyone has checked in, so I've spoken to Crystal and Duke. Your cousins Julie, Dalton and Camden needed to hear that you were going to be okay directly from me or they threatened to walk off their jobs."

Abi smiled at the image of her clan charging into the hospital.

"Once they were reassured that you would be fine, they requested a call the minute you were up to talking," he said, handing over her phone. "They also requested an update the second your eyes opened. Should you do the honors?"

Staring at the phone in the palm of her hand, she fired off a quick message to ease everyone's concerns. With everything else going on with the family, she wanted to put their minds at ease as soon as possible.

"What about Reprehensible?" she asked, gripping the phone tighter. "By now you must know his story."

"The haircuts were the first indicator, but Nathan Cruz was dressing his victims to look like a male," Grayson began. "Nathan was a grad student who was kicked out due to aggressive behavior toward his students as a teaching assistant. Turns out, he spent his childhood being taunted and tortured by his half brother."

Abi cringed. There was no excuse for the pain and devastation Nathan had inflicted on individuals and their families, but the worst felons had stories that started with intense abuse at an early age.

"Nathan's mother was a single parent who was barely able to keep food on the table," Grayson continued. "She crossed the border into Reynosa to beg for money when she was in between jobs. The woman was doing everything she could to provide for the boys who came from different fathers."

"Families make such an impact on individuals," she surmised, grateful for the amazing siblings, cousins and grandparents who'd given her love and encouragement. She might have lost her mother and never had a father, but she'd been surrounded by love. It made all the difference.

Grayson nodded before continuing, "The perp's half brother came home after living out on a rig for years when he lost his temper on their mother, accidentally killing her before turning the gun on himself."

"That's awful," Abi said, unable to even begin to process what that might do to a young mind.

"Nathan is intelligent," Grayson pointed out. "Genius IQ, in fact."

"Most true geniuses can't tie their own shoelaces," she stated. "I always saw that kind of genius as being given extra in one area at the cost of having something taken away."

"I couldn't agree more," Grayson said. After a thoughtful pause, he continued, "Nathan became aggressive with any student who resembled his half brother following the tragedy."

"Since his half brother wasn't around to punish, he had to find other people to punish and make it look random," she surmised.

"That's right," Grayson confirmed.

A nurse interrupted the conversation. She took vitals, checked machines and then provided a menu. Before leaving, she told Abi how to request a meal.

Now that Grayson had made sure Abi was going to be fine, he had a life to get home to and a child waiting.

She set the menu down and took in a deep breath. What she had to say to Grayson couldn't wait. If he rejected her, she'd rather rip the Band-Aid off now.

# Chapter Twenty-Two

"I guess we can finally put the case to rest," Abi said. Was that supposed to be Grayson's cue to leave?

Because what he had to say couldn't wait.

"I'm not planning on leaving," Grayson said to her. His heart thundered in his chest. His palms were suddenly soaked.

"What about Collin?" she asked.

"Martha is staying over for the time being," he confirmed. Finding the words to convey how he felt wasn't easy. Fear of being rejected knocked on the door.

But walking away without knowing if Abi felt the same way would be much worse even though this was a dead end. Abi didn't do kids. He had Collin.

"There's something I need to tell you," he said, after scrounging up the courage. "I've fallen in love with you even though I'm fully aware that nothing can ever come of it because I have a kid and, well, you've admitted several times to not being able to stand kids."

"That's where you're wrong, Grayson," she stated, giving him a tiny speck of hope. Was it dangerous? Because he couldn't put Collin through another loss like the one he'd suffered when Michelle died. "That little boy wriggled into my heart the moment I saw him sitting on the floor playing with his toys. Then, he talked to me and cemented the deal."

Warmth spread through Grayson's chest. Was it possible they could become a family?

"I know it's early and from the outside looking in it must seem like we barely know each other," she continued. "But I'm in love with you, Grayson. I've fallen hard and fast, and I don't want to be apart ever again." She paused before adding, "Is that too much, too soon?"

Grayson took her hand in his, "I never believed in love at first sight until you, Abi. And I've fallen hard." He was experienced enough to know the difference between infatuation and the real deal. This was it. His heart wanted Abi. "Abi Remington, I love you. And it's complicated but there's no one else in the world I want to figure life out with aside from you."

Tears streamed down Abi's cheeks as she nodded. "It's only ever been you. I never saw myself being in love with anyone let alone having a family. But I see those things with you, Grayson. I see a future that I never dreamed to imagine. I didn't think I had it in me but, it turns out, my heart was waiting for you."

He took a knee beside her bed. "Then, my next question comes easy. Will you become my equal partner in life? The person I can't wait to come home to every night? The person I'll sit on the porch and wait for until you come home every night?" He paused. "What I'm asking is… will you marry me?"

Abi's eyes sparkled as she smiled. "With all my heart, yes." And then a twinkle sparked in her eye. "I would very much like to be Collin's mother someday. I'll never replace Michelle, and I wouldn't want to, because I, of all people, know how important it is for Collin to hear the stories about Michelle. To grow up loving his mother with all his heart and, someday, understand the sacrifice she made to give him life."

Now tears welled in Grayson's eyes.

"My promise to Collin is to love him as though he is my own, but give him room to love his mother first," Abi said. "To keep her memory alive out of my love for him."

"You are an amazing person, Abi Remington," Grayson said. "And I'm the luckiest person in the world to get to be the one to love you."

The family Grayson had stopped believing would be possible was finally here. He would always have a special place in his heart for Michelle. A piece of him would always miss her. But he couldn't bring her back. Instead, she lived on in their son.

Collin would know his mother through pictures and stories. Abi had shown Grayson how important that was to a kid.

"Since we need Collin's approval to make this official, think we should have him come to the hospital?" Abi asked.

"I have an idea," he said, grabbing his cell. He made a call to Martha's voice using a video app. She answered on the second ring. "Do you mind putting Collin on the call?"

"Not a bit," Martha said.

A second later, his sweet face filled the screen.

"Hey, buddy," Grayson started. "Remember how you asked Abi to be your Mommy?"

"Yeah. Yeah." Collin chanted.

"I have great news," Grayson said through the excitement. "She said yes."

Collin lost his cool in the way only a kid could do. He jumped up and down. Excitement burst out of him.

When Martha finally had him settled again, it was her face on the screen next to his. "If I heard that correctly, I couldn't be happier for the both of you. Collin and I want to be the first to congratulate you."

"Thank you," Abi chimed in. More of those tears stained her cheeks.

Grayson ended the call before feathering kisses on her face. "I can't wait to start forever with you, Abi."

"Forever starts now," she said. "If you're up for the challenge, that is."

"I'm up for anything as long as you're with me," he quipped.

She shot him a mischievous look. "Oh, really? Because we have yet to tell my family the news."

"I hate to tell you, my love, but I asked for your hand in marriage before I proposed," he said with a grin.

"Well, then, we need to get me out of this hospital so we can start the honeymoon," Abi said with the kind of smile that wrapped him in love.

Together with Abi and Collin, he was ready to face the world—a world that finally gave him the family he'd never known he craved.

*One week later*

ABI SAT WITH her hands in her lap, tapping her foot on the tile in the headmistress's office.

Headmistress Evelyn Chin, an elegant woman, entered the room and then took her seat across from Abi and Grayson. The office had framed pictures of various geniuses hung on the walls. The furniture was simple but sophisticated. Several impressive degrees were in frames to one side of the office. The color palette was calming, and the place had an inviting feel. Toys meant to evaluate intelligence were in the adjacent play area. Abi wondered if she would pass muster.

"Thank you for waiting," Dr. Chin said before clasping her hands and placing them on top of her desk.

"No problem, Dr. Chin," Abi conceded.

Waiting for Collin's evaluation results along with whether he would be accepted into the school had Abi's stomach churning. Grayson reached over and took Abi's hand. She realized he was just as nervous as she was.

Dr. Chin looked from Grayson to Abi and back. "I don't have to tell you how impressive your son's intelligence is."

No, she didn't. But it was a good place to start.

Playing it cool, Abi nodded and smiled.

"Collin is a loving child, who takes in the world with an inquisitive eye," Dr. Chin continued.

Was this her version of hyping them up before letting them down? Because the hype had Abi praying Collin was about to be given good news.

"After spending time with your son and allowing him a chance to shadow one of our students, I'm pleased to offer Collin a place in our school," Dr. Chin said. "There's a catch, though."

The brief moment of excitement died with the qualification.

"And that is?" Abi asked. Grayson's hand squeezed hers tighter.

"One of our students is moving and their spot is open next week," Dr. Chin. "If Collin can take it, his admission is guaranteed."

"Not a problem," Abi said as she felt the relief in Grayson's hand. "Collin can start tomorrow."

Dr. Chin stood up, smiled and offered a handshake.

"Good. Because he indicated to one of the teachers that he never wanted to leave."

Abi couldn't hold back her smile. Collin was smart, inquisitive, and more than ready to leave his old school behind.

She couldn't wait for her and Grayson to tell him the news.

"Your son is waiting for you in the lobby with one of our student aides," Dr. Chin said.

*Your son.* Abi liked the sound of those words. Now that Collin's school situation was straightened out, she could head back to the hospital to be with her grandparents. And the hope they, too, would wake up soon.

\* \* \* \* \*

**HARLEQUIN**
Reader Service

# Enjoyed your book?

Try the perfect subscription for Romance readers and get more great books like this delivered right to your door.

See why over 10+ million readers have tried Harlequin Reader Service.

**Start with a Free Welcome Collection with free books and a gift—valued over $20.**

Choose any series in print or ebook. See website for details and order today:

## TryReaderService.com/subscriptions

RSBPA24R